GREG JAMES &

THE KID WHO FELL THROUGH TIME

Illustrated by ERICA SALCEDO

PUFFIN

PUFFIN BOOKS

UK | USA | Canada | Ireland | Australia
India | New Zealand | South Africa

Puffin Books is part of the Penguin Random House group of companies
whose addresses can be found at global.penguinrandomhouse.com.

www.penguin.co.uk www.puffin.co.uk www.ladybird.co.uk

First published 2025

001

Text design by Sarah Malley
Set in 12/18.2pt Baskerville MT Pro by Jouve (UK), Milton Keynes

Printed in Great Britain by Clays Ltd, Elcograf S.p.A.

The authorized representative in the EEA is Penguin Random House Ireland,
Morrison Chambers, 32 Nassau Street, Dublin D02 YH68

A CIP catalogue record for this book is available from the British Library

ISBN: 978-0-241-47057-2

All correspondence to:
Puffin Books
Penguin Random House Children's
One Embassy Gardens, 8 Viaduct Gardens, London SW11 7BW

Penguin Random House is committed to a sustainable future for our business, our readers and our planet. This book is made from Forest Stewardship Council® certified paper.

CONTENTS

When in Rome 1

When Are We? 19

Magic Puppy Paper 33

A for Angus 47

Cheesy Pleases 57

The Sunken City 75

The Oldest Cheese in the World 87

The Wonky Wheel 103

Unexpected Egyptian in Bagging Area 125

Welcome to the Ninety-Ninth Century 147

The Age of the Idiot 169

Stuck in the Past 193

The Great Dungeon Rescue 209

Shopping for Heroes 227

Marge's Time Army 243

The Cheese Chariot 257

Kragg to the Future 269

Kragg's Triumph 283

You and Halloumi Got a Whole Lot of History 293

Back to the Past 307

‘The past is a foreign country;

they have really interesting cheese there.’

Marge

CHAPTER 1

WHEN IN ROME

Angus had never been very interested in history until he visited it by accident one Tuesday night.

What?

Yes, you read that correctly. Something interesting happened on a Tuesday night. Amazing, we know. Nothing good ever normally happens on a Tuesday. But this particular Tuesday, against all odds, something did. We strongly suggest you read on and find out all about it. ***Ready?***

With a furious roar, the Roman soldier unsheathed his sword and ran full tilt towards Angus with a murderous look in his eyes.

Argh! No, wait, that's not right. We've gone too far forward. Rewind a bit.

Angus leapt into the air with fright as the rumbling noise behind him grew to a deafening volume and a shrill voice cried, 'LOOK OUT!'

Mmmm. No, that's still not it. And that's the big problem with telling a story about travelling through time. It's really, really difficult to know the best place to begin. You see, some of this story takes place in the present day. Some of it takes place far, far in the future (when our books are rightly hailed as classics). And a lot of it takes place in the very distant past. We need to be careful to get things in the right order, or it won't make any sense. Perhaps we'd better start with something incredibly boring. You know, just to set the scene before we get to the laser guns and the Ancient Egyptians and the other really cool stuff. Let's open the story with some history homework.

So, here's our hero, Angus Roberts, sitting down one Tuesday night to do his history homework. Angus wasn't very interested in history. But it was a bit more than that. History was his absolute least favourite subject at school. He simply couldn't get his head around why he had to learn all this stuff. Angus just couldn't understand why anyone was bothered about what Queen Boudicca, to pluck a name out of thin air, had done to some random Romans hundreds of years ago. It all just seemed like lists of dusty, mouldy old facts and dates to Angus – it was very hard to imagine these were real people.

To make things even worse, his history teacher was very keen on getting her students to stand up and present their work in front of the whole class – and if there was one thing that Angus hated more than history, it was presentations. Standing up to deliver a speech in front of his schoolmates made his legs feel like they'd been replaced with half-deflated balloon animals.

This particular night he'd been struggling with a piece of history homework that he found so baffling and ridiculous it made him want to ***scream***. With his pen poised at the top of a blank sheet of paper, he read the question again as the daylight faded outside his bedroom window:

How do you think ordinary people in Britain would have felt about the Romans in the years after the invasion? Imagine a conversation with one of them – what might they say? Have the Romans made their life better or worse? It's time to use your imagination!

The homework had been set earlier that day by his teacher, Ms Bancroft. She was friendly and funny and very keen on bringing history to life for her students. But, however hard Ms Bancroft tried, history just would not come to life for Angus. Something inside his brain simply refused to be interested in things that had happened hundreds of years ago. ***What was the point?*** He shook his head slowly and stared out of the window across the darkening garden. *Roman Britain.* He snorted with frustration. Who cared what some long-dead villager thought about some long-dead Romans? What could it possibly matter to him, now, today? *It's not even like they're real people*, he thought to himself angrily. *They're just piles of* *bones somewhere deep underground. Who cares what they felt, or thought? It's all gone forever.*

A small whimpering noise derailed his angry train of thought. The family's dog, McQueen, had wandered into his bedroom and was looking up at him with beseeching eyes. McQueen had been named by Angus's dad after an actor in an old film called *The Great Escape* – for the simple reason that he was always trying to ***run away***. The small brown mongrel was constantly scanning for a chance to slip out of the door or underneath the garden gate. If you took him off his lead during a walk he would vanish into any nearby forest or across a field with a delighted bark. Sometimes it took hours to track him down; he just loved running off and being free.

'I can't take you out now, boy,' said Angus sadly. 'I've got to finish this ridiculous question. And start it, for that matter. Don't suppose you know anything about Romans, do you?' McQueen whined, and placed a soft paw on his leg. 'No, of course you don't,' Angus went on, 'and no wonder. Who'd want to waste their time writing about what people who died a billion years ago thought? It's so stupid.' And, making a sudden decision, he threw down his pen and puffed out his cheeks. Maybe a bit of fresh air would clear his head, which at the moment felt like it was stuffed with hot hamster bedding rather than intelligent thoughts about life in Roman Britain. 'Come on, then,' he said, getting to his feet. 'I can always tell her you ate my homework, I suppose.'

McQueen responded with a delighted ***yip*** and capered round in circles as Angus found his coat on the back of the door and headed downstairs. 'I'm taking McQueen out for a wee!' he shouted through the living-room door. His mum, as usual, was sitting at the dining table, which was strewn with books and piles of paper. She was going for a big promotion at work and spent all her spare moments studying for the tests she'd have to take to get the new job. At his shout she gave him a distracted wave, adjusting her glasses with her other hand to pore more closely over a thick book full of figures.

'Dad!' Angus called out. 'I'm taking McQueen for a walk!' His dad had arrived home from his job absolutely exhausted, having left for work that morning before it was light. Nothing was visible of him except the bottom of his paint-spattered jeans and his feet, propped up on the coffee table in front of the sofa. A faint snore told Angus that he had fallen asleep, as the TV in front of him showed a documentary about archaeology.

'And this,' said the long-haired presenter, who was kneeling in a muddy ditch and holding up a small piece of dirty pottery, 'gives us a ***really exciting*** insight into how people lived in Roman Britain!' Angus made a rude face at him.

'Done your homework?' asked his mum, looking up briefly from her studying.

'Erm, yep. Pretty much,' replied Angus, winking at McQueen as he clipped on the lead and unlatched the front door. 'See you in a bit.' He closed the door, cutting off the TV presenter's excited voice saying in a half-whisper: 'You can really feel a powerful sense of what life must have been like all those years ago.'

'Who cares what life was like *all those years ago*,' said Angus to himself in frustration as he crossed the road towards the large park opposite his house, McQueen pulling on his lead in excitement. Street lights threw an unwholesome orangey glow over the trees and bushes, casting dark nets of shadow across a wide stretch of lawn surrounded by benches and bins. 'Go on, then,' Angus told the dog, bending down and unfastening his lead. 'Hurry up and do what you've got to do, then let's get back home.' But as soon as he was released, McQueen did what he always did in these situations. With a delighted bark, he **sprinted** off across the grass and vanished into the dim undergrowth on the other side of the lawn. Angus, who – if we're honest – had been expecting this and was keen to waste as

much time as possible so he wouldn't have to do his homework, took off in pursuit.

On the other side of the park was a small narrow road that led to the car park at the rear of the local Hyper-Buy supermarket. As Angus approached, puffing and sweating, he was just in time to see McQueen's feathery brown tail vanishing through the wide gap at the bottom of the locked gates. 'Oi!' shouted Angus. 'They're ***closed!***

We can't go shopping now! Come back!' But there was no answer except for the distant pattering of claws on concrete. With a sigh, Angus dropped to the floor and rolled underneath the gates himself. During the day the road and the car park were always packed with cars, but at this time in the evening the place was deserted. Angus got to his feet inside the gates and looked up the steep slope towards the back doors of the shop, which were in darkness. Only a couple of street lamps cast pools of light on to the rows of empty parking spaces. There was no sign of the dog.

'McQueen,' hissed Angus in a stage whisper. There was something slightly **creepy** about the empty car park, which stopped him calling out too loudly. Rows of shopping trolleys could be seen arranged beneath plastic shelters, clipped together by short chains that gave a faint rattling noise in the breeze. A few trees outside the high brick walls cast eerie moving shadows that gave the unnerving impression that someone was moving in the darkness up by the back entrance to the shop. 'McQueen!' he repeated slightly more desperately, beginning to climb slowly up the hill and peering into the half-darkness. 'Where are you, boy? What are you doing in here?' He felt a further prickle of anxiety as his eyes detected another flicker of movement up by the doors – what if there were security guards who patrolled the car park by night?

'**Here**, **boy!**' he said more loudly still. And this time there was a short answering bark from halfway up the slope. Angus saw a small, dark shape flit past the uppermost street lamp, and headed towards it on tiptoe.

McQueen was capering round and round the lamp post, wagging his tail as if he'd done something hugely clever. 'Got you!' said Angus in triumph, grabbing him by the collar and lifting him up. But at that point something very unexpected happened. While Angus had been creeping up on his dog like a stealthy panther with slippers on, he had failed to notice the peculiar noise that had begun to fill the air. It was a **rumbling**, rattling noise, and it was coming from the top end of the car park, right beside the closed and darkened automatic doors of the supermarket. The same place where those creepy moving shadows had been unnerving him just a few moments before. And now that he'd grabbed the dog, Angus suddenly realized that the rattling noise was becoming louder and louder. Something was coming.

Glancing to his right, Angus was alarmed to see a large, shadowy shape approaching through the gloom. 'What on earth is *that*?' he squeaked to himself in a scared whisper. The ***metallic clattering*** was now filling his ears as the shape loomed even closer, rocking crazily from side to side as it careened down the steep tarmac of the car park, heading right for him. What on earth was it? It was too small to be a car – and besides, cars had headlights. But whatever it was, it was about to crash right into him. Clasping McQueen tightly, Angus turned away and broke into a panicked sprint, pumping his legs and puffing out his cheeks as he flailed frantically away down the hill towards the car-park gates. But it was no use – the shape was gaining on him too fast. Angus leapt into the air with fright as the rumbling noise behind him grew to a deafening volume and a shrill voice cried,

'LOOK OUT!'

It just so happened that Angus was running past one of the dim street lights that cast a puddle of faint light beneath it. And just before the shape hit him squarely in the small of his back, he was able to cast a split-second glance back over his shoulder and see exactly what was racing down the hill towards him. What he saw was so odd that for quite some time his brain simply refused to process it. And it was this:

The kindly lady who ran the cheese counter inside Hyper-Buy was rolling towards him down the steeply sloped car park, crouched in a large metal shopping trolley.

Yes, ***that's right***. You didn't read that sentence wrong. And just to prove it, here it is again.

The kindly lady who ran the cheese counter inside Hyper-Buy was rolling towards him down the steeply sloped car park, crouched in a large metal shopping trolley.

See?

The lady's name was Marge, and Angus recognized her from his many shopping trips, both with his parents and – more recently – on his own. She hadn't been working at the supermarket that long, perhaps a year. She was generally regarded as slightly weird and eccentric because she dressed in a selection of mismatched bright colours and greeted people with a strange, double-handed gesture – waggling her hands outwards as if she was pretending to be a small bird instead of using the more conventional single-handed upward-pointing wave. But people were willing to tolerate her slightly odd ways because, it was generally agreed, she ran the most incredible cheese counter in the country – if not the entire world. It even had a name – ***Marge's Fromages*** – and within months of it opening, people were making journeys from far and wide to visit this branch of Hyper-Buy to stock up on cheeses that nobody had ever tried before.

People just couldn't understand how Marge managed to fill her display with such a varied selection of interesting cheeses – and no matter how many times they asked, she would never say where they came from. Marge was small, with long curly hair and large plastic glasses. And even though she was considered a little odd, she was still the last person you'd ever expect to be rolling down a steep hill in a shopping trolley. (We're not sure who the first person you'd expect to be doing that would be, but she was definitely the last.)

With a startled '***Welp!***' Angus fell backwards into the trolley, still holding the small brown dog to his chest. The trolley gathered speed as it continued to rattle down the hill, clanking and shaking.

'What on earth do you think you're doing?' asked Marge as Angus flailed on his back in front of her. Rather than her usual supermarket tabard, she was wearing a T-shirt with a pink-and-purple striped pattern. She was seated comfortably at the back of the trolley with her legs crossed, gripping the metal sides as the trolley continued to gather speed.

'I might ask you the same question!' countered Angus, struggling up on to his knees. 'Why are you rolling down the car park in a trolley?'

'Just visiting one of my suppliers,' replied Marge matter-of-factly. Angus, whose brain was still struggling to cope with the concept of falling backwards into a shopping trolley in a car park at night, couldn't even begin to speculate about what that sentence might mean. Instead, he made a small, confused noise, which swiftly turned into a ***loud*, *alarmed noise*** as he looked ahead to see the high brick wall at the lower end of the car park approaching them at a frighteningly fast pace.

'Prepare for temporal leap,' said a new voice from the back of the trolley. It was a calm female voice, and Angus cricked his neck really quite badly as he flailed his head

around to see who had spoken. Apart from Marge, there was nobody else there.

'**Though if you're not prepared now,**' the voice went on, '**you haven't really got much time, cos it's happening in, like, three seconds.**'

'Who said that?' shrieked Angus above the rattling of plastic wheels on concrete, which was now deafeningly loud. Finding a shopping trolley hurtling towards you is pretty hard to process. A *talking* shopping trolley . . . well, that's proper fry-your-brain stuff. McQueen, sensing Angus's confusion, whimpered and squirmed in his arms.

'**Optimal velocity achieved,**' continued the calm voice. '**Hold on to your butts, kids. Here . . . we . . . go!**' And then something odd happened. Even odder than a talking shopping trolley. Instead of ***slamming hard*** into the brick wall, which to be honest Angus hadn't been looking forward to much, the metal framework of the trolley began to glow bright silver.

Small sparks ran up and down the sides, and there was a strange, growing noise like the rushing of a high wind. Just as this noise was building to a crescendo, there was a blinding flash of bright light and the wall, the car park, the street lights and everything else ***vanished***.

CHAPTER 2

WHEN ARE WE?

Angus, who had been knocked over on to his back by the flash of light, half-opened one eye experimentally. Above him, he could see nothing but a vast expanse of swirling light in tasteful shades of dark blues and purples. Instead of the rattling of the trolley's wheels, there was no sound except for a faint, tinkling music overlaid with what sounded suspiciously like whale song. 'Where are we?' he asked shakily, sitting up.

'This is the ***chill-out zone***,' said Marge, rummaging in her pocket. 'Jelly baby?' She pulled out a crumpled paper bag and offered it to him.

'Er . . . thanks!' Angus rummaged in the bag for an orange one – his favourite. (Even when something completely unfathomable has happened, it's hard to turn down a jelly baby.) 'So – sorry,' he said, shaking his head slightly to clear it. 'The chill-out zone?'

'That's right,' she replied airily. 'I find it helps to stop people completely freaking out about what happens next.'

'And, er . . .' Angus peered over the edge of the trolley. The swirling lights were underneath them as well – the trolley appeared to be flying through nothingness. 'What *does* happen next?' he asked uneasily.

'This,' Marge told him. And, with another flash of ***blinding light***, the swirling patterns and the calming music disappeared. Instead, the shopping trolley was flying over a landscape of bright green hills in the dazzling sunshine. Angus gasped in shock, drawing in a lungful of air so fresh and cool that it felt like coming up for breath after being underwater. His eyes stung and watered as he peered wildly around, questions filling his head too fast for any of them to reach his mouth. The trolley was descending sharply, heading for a patch of undergrowth on the hillside. Beyond was a small town surrounded by wooden walls.

Smoke from the chimneys rose straight up into the still air, and Angus thought he could make out the glint of sunlight on metal beside the tall gates. But before he had time to look more closely, the trolley had landed on the grassy hillside, ***barrelled*** into the bushes and tipped over, spilling him, Marge and McQueen out on to the ground.

For a moment, Angus lay there with his eyes closed. There was a lot to take in, and he needed a few seconds to get started on the process. Firstly, there was the obvious question:

Why had the nice lady from the cheese counter been speeding about the car park at night in a shopping trolley?

And then the questions got weirder still.

Questions like this:

Why hadn't they crashed into the brick wall, which only a second before had been right in front of them?

Why was he now lying on what felt like soft grass rather than the concrete car park? In fact, where on earth were they?

And perhaps most confusingly, had that disembodied voice from the trolley really used the phrase 'hold on to your butts'?

Realizing it wasn't going to be possible to answer all – if any – of these questions with his eyes shut, he opened them, shielding them with a hand against the glare of the sun. And this is what he saw:

Behind him on the grassy slope, Marge was just getting to her feet and setting the shopping trolley back on its wheels. In front of them, away to the left, was the neatly laid-out village he'd seen from the air, with smoke rising from the chimneys. The noise of clip-clopping hooves met his ears, and a riot of birdsong from a large patch of trees close behind.

'***Temporal leap achieved***,' said the calm voice, which still seemed to be coming from the shopping trolley even though it was now completely empty. '**Welcome to**

the second century, as they used to call it in your day. Who are you, anyway?'

Angus opened his mouth to say something, but then realized there were still too many thoughts jostling for position at the front of his brain and he didn't know which one to give voice to first. Instead, he settled for a small bleating noise, which was no help to anybody.

'**Does he not talk?**' said the voice from the shopping trolley. '**Does he just make *sheep noises?***'

'Give him a chance, Hattie,' said Marge, pushing the trolley into the bushes and beginning to place fallen branches in front of it. 'He's a bit new to all this. Anyway –' she turned to Angus and planted her hands on her hips – 'Hattie's got a point. Who are you? I've seen you skulking around the supermarket.'

'I'm Angus,' said Angus, 'and I wasn't skulking, I was shopping.' This was true. More often than not recently, Angus had ended up volunteering to do the shopping for his over-tired and busy parents.

'Fair enough,' said Marge, 'but that doesn't explain what you were doing in the car park in the middle of the night, does it?'

'I was looking for my dog,' Angus replied truthfully, holding up McQueen as evidence. The brown mongrel gave a small 'a-woo' as if confirming the story.

'**Ooh, he does talk,**' said the voice from the trolley. '**And so does the dog. Cool!**'

'Well, Angus, you'll just have to come with me on my shopping trip,' Marge decided, pursing her lips. 'Nothing else for it. Then you can go home and ***keep your mouth shut***, all right?' She turned back to the trolley and pulled a large tote bag out of it.

'But, but . . .' Angus gestured around at the sunlit landscape.

'No time to answer all the questions now,' Marge replied.

'**She's right,**' said the calm female voice. '**Return leap set for twenty-eight minutes and fifty seconds. So you'd better start *roamin'* around.**'

'Oh, very good,' said Marge. 'You're getting better at those.'

'What,' asked Angus faintly, 'is going on? Where are we?'

'**I knew he'd ask that,**' said the voice from the shopping trolley. '**Completely the wrong question.**'

Angus looked over his shoulder at the village as a cart pulled by two large oxen left the gates and began to trundle down a wide, flat stone road. 'The real question,' Marge told him, 'is *when* are we?'

'***When*** are we?' echoed Angus blankly.

'I just told you,' replied the trolley. **'AD 212. Hence my clever joke about Romans. *Roamin'* around? Get it?'**

'Romans,' Angus repeated faintly.

'Is he just going to keep repeating everything we say?' asked the trolley.

'He'll get used to it,' said Marge in a soothing voice. 'Come on,' she told Angus, beckoning to him as she began to stride off down the hill towards the village, slinging the hessian tote bag over her shoulder. 'You can come shopping with me, just this once, then I'll drop you home. We haven't got long, though, so don't dawdle.'

Not surprisingly, Angus's brain was having a hard time keeping up with what was going on. It had started off with the obvious thought: *I must be dreaming.* But this was clearly not a dream. For a start, light rain was soaking through his coat, and you don't usually get wet during a dream unless you knock over the water next to your bed. And secondly, he hadn't been ***asleep*** when these strange events had started – and being asleep is generally considered the minimum requirement for a dream to occur. At this point his brain decided – wrongly – that it might help if he stammered and gibbered a little bit.

'B-b-b–' stammered Angus. 'Keth . . . feth . . . wuh?'

'Stop stammering and gibbering,' said Marge over her shoulder. She was already quite a distance away, striding off down the hill. Angus, deciding that whatever was going on, he didn't want to deal with it on his own, scuttled after her. Marge was moving surprisingly quickly towards the gates, and he had to break into an awkward half-jog to catch up with her. 'What did you mean, *when* are we?' he said, panting as he grew closer. 'And why can your shopping trolley talk? And why is it daytime?'

'Isn't it ***obvious?***' she replied bafflingly, waving to a figure who was standing near the gates leaning on a long rake. As they came nearer, Angus could see that it was a tall, broad-shouldered man dressed in rough trousers and a blue tunic.

'*Dy da, Marge ma koweth!*' said the man, smiling warmly at Marge before turning a curious eye on to Angus. '*Desh anouth da welet merkett?*'

'Muh?' Angus gaped at him. 'What?'

'What's the matter?' Marge grinned at him. 'Is your Brittonic not quite up to scratch, dear? Try these.' She rummaged in a pocket and pulled out a small earpiece, like a single headphone, made of the same plastic as her glasses. Unthinkingly, Angus stuck it in his right ear.

'*Piv e kila?*' the man was now saying. But, as the earpiece went in, Angus heard the same soft female voice that had spoken from the shopping trolley talking inside his head.

'***Decoding and translating* target language – early twenty-first-century English. Stand by,**' said the voice, followed by a short fizzing noise.

'And who's your young friend?' Angus heard the voice clearly, though it didn't match up to the movements of the tall man's mouth.

'Hello, Dillion,' said Marge, and Angus turned to look at her. She was smiling sweetly at the man. 'This is a friend of mine. Angus, meet Dillion. He runs the best cheese stall in this entire ***century***.' Angus looked from one to the other in confusion. He had the unsettling impression that he was watching a film that had been dubbed from a foreign language. Because, although he was hearing both Marge and this man Dillion speaking in English, the way their lips were moving made it quite clear that they were, in fact, talking in some other language – presumably the one he'd heard Dillion using before he'd put in this strange earpiece.

'**It takes a bit of getting used to,**' said the calm voice in his head. '**I'm translating for you. You wouldn't get very far otherwise. Give it a try.**'

Angus opened his mouth to say: 'Hello, pleased to meet you.' But instead he found completely different words coming out of his mouth – something that sounded to him like: '***Doodah***, ***ferry anarchy toffee apple***.' It seemed to please Dillion, though. Grinning beneath his untidy mop of dark, shaggy hair, the man held out a large, calloused hand for Angus to shake before leaning his rake against a wooden fence and beckoning them to follow him as he headed towards the main gates of the town.

'This way, then,' he called over his shoulder. 'Menneth will be pleased to see you.'

'What on earth is going on?' asked Angus in an undertone, jogging to catch up with Marge as she trotted merrily after Dillion towards the wooden gates. 'How come I can talk to that man? And where are we, anyway?'

'Hattie's translating for you,' Marge replied. 'I thought that was obvious. And she already told you where we are – didn't you pay attention? This is the year AD 212.'

'And . . . what are we doing here, exactly?' asked Angus weakly. By now they had reached the gates. Spread out

before them was a neatly arranged settlement, with sturdily built wooden buildings lining a wide, stone-flagged road. Visible ahead was a large open space in the centre of the village, with brightly coloured cloth awnings flapping in the warm breeze above the heads of the crowd.

'I told you, I'm just here to pick up some cheese,' replied Marge. 'Now, don't draw too much attention to yourself, will you? They don't pay us much mind – they're used to people dressed in unusual ways. But you don't want to give them an excuse to start asking too many ***awkward questions***.'

'Who are *they*, exactly?'

In reply, Marge took him gently by the shoulder and pointed down the street. There, among the passers-by in their colourful cloth garments, were a group of fully armoured Roman soldiers, looking for all the world as if they'd just stepped out of a history textbook.

CHAPTER 3

MAGIC PUPPY PAPER

Angus couldn't stop himself ***gasping in shock*** as he stared at the Roman soldiers' shining armour and plumed helmets.

'Try not to gasp in shock, dear,' Marge told him kindly. 'It's a dead giveaway. Just act casual.' Angus wasn't quite sure how he was supposed to act casual, almost two thousand years into the past. It's not something that happens on your average evening. He affected a kind of sauntering, bandy-legged walk, which earned him a suspicious glance from one of the legionaries as they wandered past, exchanging nods and greetings with some of the passers-by.

'What are you doing?' hissed Marge as Angus's floppy leg landed in a puddle.

'Acting casual, like you told me,' he whispered back.

'I said act ***casual***, not pretend to be drunk,' she told him before tutting. 'Just keep quiet while I do the shopping and we'll be out of here.' By now they were in the main square. Angus turned on the spot, trying to take it all in. More Roman soldiers were now visible here and there, mingling with the crowds or bartering at some of the many stalls that lined the area, selling a bewildering variety of goods and produce. The crowd parted to let a small cart drawn by a large, ponderous ox move past. The cart was piled with hay, tied into neat bundles, and two children were perched on the back. One of them, a girl, gave Angus a shy wave as they passed, and without thinking he waved back, earning himself a small smile from her tanned and grubby face in reply.

'Come on,' Marge told him, 'we can't hang about flirting. The Time Trolley will be returning before very long. Let's load up and ship out.'

'*Time* Trolley?' Angus repeated.

Marge nodded.

'Hang on.' Angus stopped in a quiet patch of the street and faced her. 'Wait a second. Are you seriously telling me that you built a time machine . . . out of a shopping trolley?'

'Well,' said Marge airily, 'I figured, if you're going to build a time machine, you might as well make sure there's plenty of room for cheese. Besides, it makes it easier to hide in your time period. There are millions of the things. Took centuries for them all to rust away.'

'A time machine . . .' repeated Angus, 'out of a ***shopping trolley?***'

'Well, what else would you make a time machine out of?'

'I dunno.' Angus thought for a second. 'I mean, almost anything else would have been better. What about a cool sports car?'

'Don't be ridiculous,' Marge snorted. 'How am I going to hide a sports car in the cheese section of Hyper-Buy? It'd stick out like a sore thumb!'

'What about a fridge, then?'

Marge patted him on the cheek. 'That's a ridiculous idea, dear,' she told him. 'Come on.' She turned and led him onward through the crowds of people in their blue and red tunics and rough leather boots. 'We don't have long.'

'**Fifteen minutes to temporal resolve,**' said the voice in his head, as if on cue.

Angus, still feeling very confused and swallowing about a thousand other questions, followed Marge towards a small stall in the corner of the square with a bright yellow awning over the top. A smiling woman behind the counter caught sight of Marge and called out to her: '***Hello**, **my friend!*** Lovely to see you again. What are you looking for today?'

As they approached, Angus could see that the neatly laid-out stall was packed with different cheeses – not unlike Marge's counter at his local supermarket. 'Those look good,' said Marge, pointing to a row of round cheeses wrapped in leaves. 'Tell me about those.' As the two women began a very in-depth dairy-based chat, Angus looked around him. It wasn't that he wasn't interested in cheese – he was as partial to a miniature wax-wrapped cheesy treat or a string of gooey mozzarella as the rest of us. He just felt that he didn't want to waste his entire time in history feeling like he was on a trip to the market with his nan.

Opposite Menneth's cheese stall was another, larger

stall with pieces of chunky jewellery laid out on a thick slab of cloth. Standing behind the stall, the vendor looked up as Angus approached. Closest to Angus was a row of thick copper bracelets and he bent over them to take a closer look. One was embossed with a letter A and he picked it up, placing it experimentally on his wrist. Behind him he could hear Marge saying, 'Ten of those then, please, dear.'

'What did you bring to barter with today?' asked Menneth eagerly. 'I hope it's the usual! We're nearly out.' At this, Angus turned to see what the Anglo-Saxon woman was talking about. *What had Marge brought from the future to exchange for goods here, in the past? What would people in history really, really want?* he thought to himself. *Medicine, perhaps? Some incredible piece of technology, like a phone? No, not a phone,* he told himself. *There's nowhere to charge it.*

Marge was rummaging in the tote bag over her shoulder. 'What are you giving them?' asked Angus breathlessly. 'Antibiotics or something?'

'No, dear,' she replied kindly. 'I always bring some of ***this*** with me into the past. Any time before the mid nineteenth century it's absolute gold dust.' And, triumphantly, she pulled an ordinary twin-pack of toilet paper out of the tote.

Menneth's eyes lit up with delight. '***Magic puppy paper!***' she said in an excited squeak. Angus peered across and saw that, sure enough, the toilet rolls had a picture of a cute fluffy pup and the words 'Puppy Soft' written in pink writing.

(**Authors' Note:** This book is a work of fiction and any resemblance to actual toilet paper, used or unused, is entirely coincidental.)

'Wait a moment,' said Angus. 'Are you really buying that cheese with loo roll?'

'Like I said, dear, it's worth its weight in gold here,' said Marge, smiling. 'I mean, think of the alternative.'

FACT PIG

HI, KIDS! It's the Fact Pig here! Your friendly, oinking guide to the fascinating world of history! I'll be popping up throughout the story with some useful info! **Oink!** Starting with some incredible facts about what Anglo-Saxons used instead of toilet paper!

Oh, gross! Is this really necessary, Fact Pig?

Yes, it is. It's **fascinating** historical knowledge.

Are you sure you're not just looking for a cheap laugh by talking about people wiping their bottoms?

No, no, absolutely not. I would never lower myself to such a level. I'm the **Fact Pig**, remember? Not just some normal pig who thinks bottoms are funny.

Sigh OK, then, Fact Pig. We give up. What did Anglo-Saxons use instead of toilet paper?

Moss.

Ewww. What, moss?

Yes, moss. It's soft and absorbent. But how did they know **someone else** hadn't already used the same patch of moss? That's what keeps me awake at night in my Fact Sty.

OK, OK, too much information. Thank you, Fact Pig. That was very informative. Off you tootle.

Goodbye, friends. Happy wiping.

'Keep it under your hat,' Marge was telling the stallholder. 'Don't want everyone hassling me. This is just between us, all right?'

Angus was pondering how nice it must be to get hold of an actual toilet roll for the first time ever, when abruptly the calm voice that Marge had called 'Hattie' broke into his wipe-based reverie. **'Ten minutes to temporal resolve. Return to the Time Trolley immediately.'**

Marge, who had been busily packing cheese into a cloth tote bag she'd pulled out of one of her pockets, beckoned to him. 'Home time, come on.'

'Leaving already?' Dillion had reappeared behind them. 'You never seem to stick around for long.'

'Oh, you know,' Marge told him airily. 'Places to go, people to see.'

'I'll walk you to the gate,' he replied, smiling.

'Come on, stowaway,' Marge told Angus, placing a firm arm around his shoulders and steering him back out of the square. 'You really don't want to miss your ride home. You'd be waiting ***forever*** for another one.'

As they walked, an idea popped into Angus's head. And he was fairly certain that this was going to be his one and only chance to put it into action. 'Just out of interest,' he asked, turning to Dillion, 'could I please ask – what do you think about the Romans?'

'The Romans?' Dillion stopped and turned towards him.

'Yes,' said Angus. 'What do you really think of them? They invaded your country, after all. Right?'

'That's an interesting way of putting it,' said Dillion, falling into step beside him as they continued towards the main gates. 'I mean, lots of people come from abroad. Take that guy, for instance.' He pointed at a short man with straggly hair and a metal helmet. 'Bloomin' Saxons, coming over here with their fancy earthworks,' Dillion went on. 'At least the Romans brought some decent wine with them. I'll tell you something not many people know about the Romans . . .'

Five minutes later, Angus was fairly certain that he had all the material he needed to write some seriously impressive history homework. Just outside the wooden gates, Marge and Dillion were shaking hands and making some very fond farewells when he heard a shout from down the road.

'THERE HE IS! STOP, THIEF!'

Three Roman guards were sprinting down the street towards them, armour clanking and the plumes on their polished helmets flapping from side to side. With a shock that felt like it had turned his entire insides to water, Angus realized he was still wearing the chunky copper bracelet with the letter A on it.

'Marge,' he said urgently, 'we may have a slight problem. I need to return this to the market stall. Right now!'

'***Two minutes* to temporal resolve,**' said Hattie inside his head – and by Marge's expression he could tell she'd heard it too.

'There isn't time!' she said, looking panicked. 'We've got to go! The trolley will leave without us.'

By now, the Roman soldiers were just metres away. 'Halt!' one of them bellowed.

'Run!' shrieked Marge at the same time, pushing Dillion away from her. He fell flat on his back into the mud, and Marge grabbed Angus by the hand and began to dash up the slope towards the bush where she'd hidden the shopping trolley. As they ran, Angus could see some of the lower branches shuddering and shaking as the time machine prepared to fire up.

'***Get them!***' bellowed the Roman soldier, unsheathing his sword and running at full tilt towards them with a murderous look in his eyes.

With only seconds to spare, Marge and Angus plunged into the bush and dived into the shopping trolley, which was glowing with a strange silver light.

And seconds later, there was a blinding flash, Angus's ears popped and he found that they were once again beneath the orange street lights of the supermarket car park.

'Well,' said Marge, clambering out of the trolley and dusting herself down. 'You won't be jumping into any more shopping trolleys in a hurry, I hope!'

'Are you kidding?' said Angus. 'That was incredible! I have so many more questions!'

'And I,' replied Marge, looking at him sternly, 'am going to answer precisely none of them. What you've seen tonight is ***top*, *top secret***. Do you understand?'

'Well, in that case I won't tell you what Dillion told me about the Romans,' Angus retorted.

'I don't care,' Marge replied. 'Tell it to your history teacher!'

'Oh, don't worry, I will.' Angus turned on his heel and, putting McQueen down and clipping on his lead, headed home. For the first time in his own history, he was actually looking forward to doing his homework.

CHAPTER 4
A FOR ANGUS

Ms Bancroft's face beamed like a freshly polished lighthouse as she held up Angus's exercise book in front of the whole class later that week. 'And the best piece of work – in fact one of the best pieces of history homework I have ***ever seen*** in my whole career – came from Angus!' she said, grinning at him delightedly.

Angus shifted uncomfortably in his hard wooden chair as the rest of the class turned to stare at him. He caught looks of confusion, jealousy and – from some of the keen kids in the front row – open hostility in their gaze. It wasn't that Angus was bad at schoolwork – he was just one of those students who tends to slip under the radar. He had never scored top marks for his homework before. This amount of attention was new and, he discovered to his surprise, he was actually quite enjoying it. 'In fact,' Ms Bancroft went on, 'Angus's history homework was so good that I'm going to ask him to share it with the whole school in assembly tomorrow!'

Panic washed over Angus like a bucket of iced wee. He hated getting up in front of his class to talk, let alone the whole school. '**NO!**' he squealed in a high-pitched voice that made his friend Frank, who was sitting next to him, give a delighted snort of laughter. 'I mean . . .' he went on, trying to get his voice back to a more normal pitch, 'I'm sure they won't like it. It's very boring, really.'

'Have more faith in yourself!' said Ms Bancroft bracingly. 'I loved your homework, and I'm sure the rest of the school will too.'

'Yeah, Angus,' said Frank, digging him in the ribs and grinning. 'We're all rooting for you. Get up there and give 'em a bit of history!'

Angus glared at him.

'That's settled, then,' said Ms Bancroft proudly. 'I'll arrange it with the head later on.'

'. . . And so that's why Dillion wasn't as angry with the Romans as you might expect,' Angus read out shakily the following morning. Out of the corner of his eye he could see the beaming face of his headteacher – Mr Peel – who was sitting cross-legged on a chair nearby and nodding at him enthusiastically with an expression of bright-eyed approval. In front of them, the upturned faces of the entire school gawped in his direction. 'In fact,' he went on, feeling a warm rush of relief as he remembered that this was the final sentence, 'he was far too busy with his market stall to worry too much about the invaders – as long as they had plenty of wine to barter with.' At this, Mr Peel gave a delighted shout of laughter, now nodding ***so violently*** that his large head seemed in danger of becoming detached from his neck. He uncoiled himself from the chair, stood up and placed a firm hand on Angus's arm, then looked around the room.

‘***Imagination!***’ he bellowed abruptly and at a surprisingly loud volume, making some of the younger kids in the front row jump. ‘That’s the ticket. Yes, yes, yes.’ His fingers tightened uncomfortably. ‘This student is an example to you all!’ he roared, shaking Angus like a rag doll. Mr Peel was one of those head teachers whose enthusiasm and volume controls are both set permanently to maximum. His large Adam’s apple shuddered with excitement like a toad trapped in a hosepipe. ‘And for that reason,’ he continued, his voice echoing back from the murals on the hall walls, ‘I am making Arthur here . . .’

‘Angus,’ hissed Ms Bancroft from her seat nearby.

‘That’s what I said,’ insisted Mr Peel, giving Angus another shake for emphasis. ‘That is why I am making Argos here our Star of the Week!’ He plucked a certificate from a nearby table and held it aloft like a magical scroll. ‘And it is also why,’ he added, ‘Ms Bancroft and I have a very special announcement to make!’

Angus caught the history teacher’s eye and was alarmed to see that she had raised her eyebrows in excitement.

'As you all know,' Mr Peel went on, 'we have the school open evening coming up towards the end of term, when your parents all see what we've been up to. And we have decided that Andrew . . . **Angus** here –' he gave him another firm shake – 'will be giving our keynote presentation to all the parents! Isn't that exciting?' Angus could think of several words to describe what it was, and 'exciting' was not one of them. It was alarming, terrifying, intimidating, horrifying and traumatizing. Definitely not exciting.

What was quite exciting, though, was the effect that his Star of the Week certificate had on his parents when he took it home that evening. In and of itself, it wasn't the most amazing award he'd ever seen. It was printed on thin card, with

STAR of the WEEK

written in large letters at the top, and Mr Peel's signature in biro at the bottom. Not especially impressive. But when he shyly plucked it from his bag and showed it to his parents after school, the result completely stunned him. For the first time in as long as he could remember, his mum actually put aside her books and notepads and leapt up from the table to have a look. His dad, who'd been snoozing on the sofa after another marathon shift, reached for the remote control and switched the TV off, turning round on the sofa to face him as he hovered at the back of the room like an awkward ghost.

'Star of the Week?' read his father, his voice breaking into a delighted squeak. 'Star? Of the whole week?'

'It's nothing, Dad,' mumbled Angus in an embarrassed undertone.

'It most certainly is not nothing,' his dad corrected him. And, vaulting over the back of the sofa with a click of tired knees, he swept Angus from the floor and spun him round with a look of pure joy on his face. 'Look at this, Liz,' he said as they twirled. 'We've got ourselves an actual shooting star.'

'*Angus's history homework was some of the best writing I've ever seen from a student at this level*,' read his mum, who'd picked the certificate up from the floor. Angus had dropped it in surprise at his dad's enthusiastic reaction. '*He showed a truly amazing ability to imagine what an actual historical character might have thought and felt – a very rare skill.* Well!' she said, beaming. 'This calls for a celebration, I'd say.'

'What about your promotion, though?' mumbled Angus. 'I thought you needed to study.'

'Some things are bigger than a silly old promotion,' his mum told him. 'And this is definitely one of them.'

'You're right!
You're absolutely right!'
Angus's dad put him down and
danced a small jig around the carpet.
'I was making fish fingers for tea, but that won't do. That won't do at all for the actual star of the entire week! Stars

don't eat fish fingers, do they? They eat pizza! As much pizza as they can manage without bursting! Go and get changed, quick! We're hitting the all-you-can eat buffet at Dough Daddy! And we're hitting it *hard*!'

Later that night, Angus lay in bed with two different but equally brilliant feelings in his tummy region. The first was the feeling of being full of pizza. And we mean really, really full of it. So full of pizza that your whole body feels like a ***giant calzone***: warm and doughy on the outside and tightly packed with melted oozy cheese and salami on the inside. It's truly one of the best feelings in the world. But alongside that was another sensation – equally melty and oozy in its way but less mozzarella-flavoured. It was a warm, glowing feeling of ***pride***. His parents hadn't been that interested in him for ages. His mum always seemed too busy and his dad was usually too tired to hear about his day. They'd never actually wanted to read a piece of his homework before.

Just as he drifted off to sleep, Angus decided two things. Firstly, that an all-you-can-eat pizza buffet is the second-best thing in the world. But secondly, that the attention and pride he'd felt from his mum and dad was actually better than pizza. Better than stuffed crust, even. Angus realized that he wanted to be Star of the Week again. Plus, he had a history presentation to prepare for. And he knew ***exactly*** how he was going to do both of those things.

CHAPTER 5

CHEESY PLEASES

The following day, after school, Angus rushed straight to Hyper-Buy. He wasn't the only one – the supermarket was a popular stop-off on the way home and the entrance was packed with dark school uniforms just like his as kids clustered round the hot-food counter, grabbing sausage rolls or cheese-and-bean slices. But Angus rushed past all of them. Running the gauntlet of swerving pushchairs and teetering trolleys, he ***sped*** through the fruit and veg aisles and raced towards the back of the store, where a series of long counters sold fish, cakes, meat and – right at the far end – cheese. As he rounded the corner by the yoghurts he could already see the sign:

Marge's Fromages, with a shock of curly hair visible underneath as Marge served a customer.

'I need your help!' gasped Angus as he approached. Marge, who was wrapping a large block of creamy yellow cheese in greaseproof paper, shot him a suspicious look.

'You'll need to take a ***ticket***, sir,' she told him through pursed lips, 'and wait your turn.' She nodded towards a small machine on the counter, which dispensed small tickets with numbers on. Angus ripped one off, then groaned to see that he was number 54, but the red numbers on the electronic board set above the cheese counter only showed 41. Hopping impatiently from foot to foot, he settled down to wait.

'What have you got today then, Marge?' boomed a voice from beside him as the indicator board flicked round to number 42. Waving his ticket, a large man in a suit stepped forward. 'Best cheese counter in the country, this,' he said to nobody in particular as he approached. 'I just don't know how she does it. That one you sold me last weekend . . .' he said to Marge, making a chef's kiss with his fingers. 'I don't think I've ever tasted anything quite so delicious.'

'Oh, yes,' said Marge. 'I remember. Yes, it's good that one, isn't it? Comes from a part of Italy that's very hard to reach.'

The besuited man frowned. 'What part of Italy is hard to reach?' he asked in confusion.

'1720,' she replied. 'But anyway –' she waved a hand – 'I'm all out of that one, I'm afraid, Graham. Need to make another trip. But I picked ***this one*** up yesterday.' She pointed, and with a rush of excitement Angus saw a block of the dark red cheese she'd picked up in Roman Britain the previous evening. 'Very interesting, this one. They don't make 'em like this any more, you know. Would you like to try?'

While Marge continued discussing cheese with her customers, Angus looked around the shop. Everything else looked completely normal, from the man handing out free samples of cake to the woman at the fresh-fish counter in her striped apron. The idea that there was – he could hardly bring himself to think the words – a time machine hidden away at the back of this perfectly ordinary supermarket was completely unbelievable. But he'd witnessed it for himself – there was no use denying it. There could be no other possible explanation.

Angus jerked out of his reverie when he realized someone was speaking. 'Number 54?' Marge was saying loudly, looking around the store. 'Who's 54?' Sighing, she prepared to press the button that would take her on to the next number.

'**No**, **no**, **noooo!**' squeaked Angus frantically, so excited to have reached the front of the queue at last that he couldn't quite get his words out properly. '***Fofty-foo!*** I mean, ***five-ty feff!*** That's me!' He scuttled up to the counter, eyes wide and face red.

'How can I help you, sir?' asked Marge, narrowing her eyes suspiciously.

'I want . . .' said Angus, lowering his voice and looking nervously around. 'I want to come time travelling again in your magic shopping trolley, please.'

'**SMOKED CHEDDAR?**' replied Marge loudly. 'Certainly, sir. Very smoky. Very delicious.' Then she leaned forward and spoke in a stern whisper. 'I thought I made this perfectly clear last night. You didn't see anything. No trolley. No time travelling. ***Nothing***. Got it? Now, scram.' With a thud she slammed a piece of cheese wrapped in clingfilm on to the counter and backed away. '55?' she shouted, pressing the button next to the till. 'Next number, please! 55!' And before he could respond, Angus had been shouldered out of the way by another customer.

*

Over the next week, Angus's parents were more than a little confused by the amount of cheese he kept bringing home. Every day without fail, he would take a ticket and wait for his turn at Marge's Fromages. When that turn came, he would plead briefly with Marge to take him time travelling again. She would deny all knowledge, insisting she had no idea what he was talking about before slamming a random piece of cheese down on the counter and turning to her next customer.

Angus was growing desperate. Ms Bancroft had started a new topic in history: Ancient Egypt. 'And I'm sure Angus is going to share some very exciting insights with us about what life might really have been like back then!' she'd told the class, her eyes glinting with enthusiasm. 'And he'll be putting some of this new knowledge into his ***big presentation*** for the parents' open evening as well!' Angus squirmed in his chair. He had absolutely no idea how he was going to put a presentation together unless Marge helped him. What was even worse was the moment that his dad asked him: 'Not Star of the Week this week?' without tearing his eyes away from the TV the following night. Ten days later, Angus was almost beside himself with frustration.

It was two full weeks before Marge cracked. The cheeses she had been handing over to Angus had been becoming progressively stinkier in an attempt to deter him – the last one had smelled like **socks full of compost** – but he refused to be put off. Clutching his numbered ticket, he would approach the counter wearing his best pleading expression. And, finally, she gave in. 'You're really not going to let this go, are you?' she asked.

'I'm really not,' Angus confirmed. 'But I only want to go once more, I swear. Honest. Please. Just one quick trip to help with my homework and this stupid presentation and I'll leave you alone.'

'Promise?' asked Marge.

'Promise,' Angus repeated.

'Swear by all that is cheesy?'

'***I swear on all the cheeses***,' he confirmed. 'Even that last one that my dad had to actually bury in the flower bed.'

Marge folded her arms and gave a deep sigh. 'Oh, all right, then,' she said grumpily. 'I can tell I'm not going to get a moment's peace otherwise. Meet me in the car park at ten o'clock.'

'I've got to be in bed at 10:30, is that OK?' Angus asked anxiously.

'Still not quite got your head around the concept of time travel?' she asked him dryly.

'Oh, yeah,' said Angus after a brief think. 'Sorry. See you later, then!' And, not wanting to give her time to change her mind, he dashed away down the cereals aisle.

'Just taking McQueen for a walk!' shouted Angus later that evening, clipping the dog's lead on and heading out of the door. '***Won't be long!***' he shouted through the letterbox, before adding a sneaky chuckle and muttering, 'Thanks to the wonders of time travel,' as he carefully crossed the road (***responsible author detail***) and cut across the park towards the rear entrance to Hyper-Buy.

As before, the car park was padlocked shut, but Angus rolled easily under the gate and jogged excitedly to the top of the hill, where he could see Marge bending over the shopping trolley.

'Here he comes,' she said as Angus approached. 'Mr Persistent.'

'This is really, really kind of you!' Angus panted, dragging McQueen along by his lead. After what had happened last time, the dog seemed reluctant to approach the trolley.

Marge gave a small harrumph but followed it with a smile. 'Remember what I told you?' she asked him, wagging a finger. 'Just this once, OK? Don't you be bothering me at the cheese counter tomorrow saying you want another go. Deal?'

'Deal,' agreed Angus.

'All right, then.' Marge straightened up, grabbing the bar at the back of the trolley and shoving it into position, facing down the slope. 'Where do you want to go?'

Angus had the answer all prepared. He needed to research his new history topic and that meant only one thing. '***Ancient Egypt***, please,' he told her.

'Whatever do you want to go *there* for?'

'Well, you know . . .' Angus remembered the

introductory lesson he'd had on the topic the previous day. 'There's pharaohs, mummies, the pyramids, sphinxes, erm . . . camels? Generally one of the most fascinating periods in all of history, ever?'

'Yes,' said Marge grudgingly. 'But a ***terrible*** cheese selection. I mean, they really only had one kind. And they made that by accident by storing milk in a cow's stomach.'

'Well, that's where I'd like to go, please, if it's no trouble.' Angus stood firm, worried suddenly that Marge would far rather just take him to another bit of the past simply because the dairy produce was more imaginative. 'Is that really the only reason you travel in time?' he asked suddenly, as the thought hit him. 'Looking for ***interesting cheese?***'

'To tell you the truth,' said Marge, lowering her voice and leaning towards him, 'I'm not really supposed to use the time machine at all. I'm supposed to be in hiding. But –' she made an embarrassed face – 'I didn't think it would do too much harm, just taking the odd shopping trip. And I do really, really like cheese.'

'Ooh.' Angus thought this sounded fascinating. 'In hiding? Why? Who are you hiding from?'

'***Too many questions***,' she replied abruptly. 'Come on, jump in. Questions are dangerous things. Remember the deal? One quick trip to Ancient Egypt and you leave me alone. Right?'

'S'pose so,' said Angus reluctantly, picking up McQueen and clambering awkwardly into the shopping trolley. 'I'd love to know who you're hiding from, though. Sounds very dramatic.'

Authors' Note:

It is indeed dramatic that Marge is in hiding, and when you find out why she's in hiding, and who from, we guarantee that you will make an excited '***ooh***' noise. But we're not going to tell you those details just yet, because we want to build up the anticipation a little bit more. We just wanted to break into the story at this point and let you know, because we realize that it is ***slightly annoying***. Almost as annoying as someone making a really silly high-pitched noise right in your ear.

EeeeeeEEEeeEEEEeeEEEEeeeeeeeee.

See, that's ***really*** annoying, isn't it?

Here it comes again. EEEEEEEeEEEEeeeeeEEEEEE.

KARK!

Hello, it's the Chief Puffin here. I'm just taking a break from sitting on this windswept clifftop with a fish in my beak because it's been brought to my attention by a passing seagull that two of my authors are wasting your valuable reading time again by breaking into the story and making annoying noises at you. If you'll wait just a second I shall deal with them.

EeeeEEEEeeEEEEEEEeeeeeee.

KARK!

SHUT UP, you pair of absolute lettuces! Stop making stupid noises and get on with the story!

Another note from the authors:

We would like to apologize to you, the reader, and also to you, the Chief Puffin, for the previous interruption. We got carried away. Now, on with the story.

KARK!

That's better. Oi, who's taken my fish?

'Pop this in,' said Marge, as she hopped neatly into the trolley behind Angus. She was holding out the earpiece he'd worn before.

'Ooh, I wanted to ask about that,' said Angus, putting it back in his ear. 'This lets me talk to Hattie, right?'

'**Oh, here we go again**,' said the calm voice in his head. '**Where are we off to this time?**'

'Who are you, anyway?' asked Angus curiously.

'**I thought Marge already told you,**' the voice replied. '**H.A.T.T.I.E. Human-Accessible Time Travel Interface Engine. I'm the onboard computer for the Time Trolley.**'

'And you can translate different languages, too?' asked Angus. 'That's super-clever.'

'**Why, thank you,**' Hattie replied.

'It's all pretty futuristic, isn't it?' said Angus, turning slightly to look at Marge.

'**Of course it's *futuristic*,**' Hattie started to say. '**After all –**'

But Marge cut her off. 'He asks too many questions, this one,' she said curtly. 'Time circuits set? Let's go. I haven't had my tea yet. One quick trip to Ancient Egypt, all right? Hattie, fire her up!'

With a jolt, the trolley began to roll forward across the car park. 'Hang on tight,' Marge told Angus. 'And keep a close eye on that ruddy dog. This place is absolutely full of cats.'

'So, why are we rolling down the hill?' Angus asked, clinging on as the trolley picked up speed.

'**The Time Trolley uses *kinetic energy* to activate the temporal leap,**' Hattie's voice told him. '**We need to achieve a certain speed in order to make the jump.**'

'When this shopping trolley reaches eight miles per hour,' shouted Marge over the clanking of the wheels, 'you're going to see some serious sphinxes.'

Suddenly, the trolley gave a violent lurch to one

side, almost tipping over. '**What's that?**' Marge shrieked.

'**One of the wheels is not functioning correctly,**' Hattie replied.

'That always happens with shopping trolleys,' Angus broke in. 'And you always think, *oh, it'll be OK, I'll be able to steer it* but you never really can. It drives my dad mad when he takes me shopping. Last time it happened he ended up knocking over an entire display of cauliflowers cos our trolley wouldn't stop steering to the left.'

'Yeah, but this isn't just a trip out for vegetables,' Marge told him tersely. 'We're about to leap thousands of years into the past. One slight error with the trolley could mean . . .'

But she never got the chance to finish the sentence. Bolts of electricity had begun to ***zig-zag*** up and down the trolley's metal sides. And with a blinding flash and a *whumph* of heat, it vanished, leaving nothing but a pair of flaming, slightly wonky tyre tracks in the empty Hyper-Buy car park.

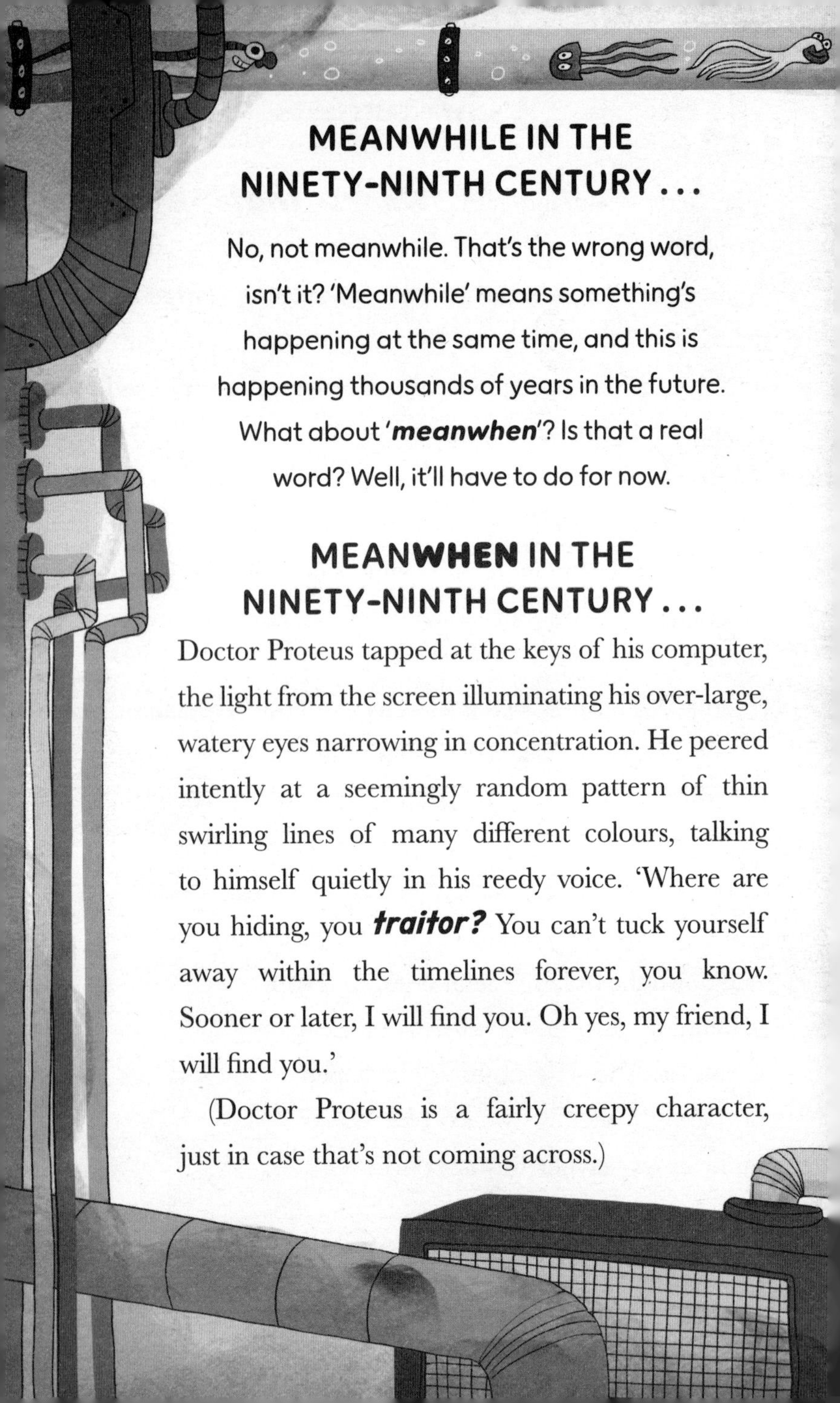

MEANWHILE IN THE NINETY-NINTH CENTURY . . .

No, not meanwhile. That's the wrong word, isn't it? 'Meanwhile' means something's happening at the same time, and this is happening thousands of years in the future. What about '***meanwhen***'? Is that a real word? Well, it'll have to do for now.

MEAN**WHEN** IN THE NINETY-NINTH CENTURY . . .

Doctor Proteus tapped at the keys of his computer, the light from the screen illuminating his over-large, watery eyes narrowing in concentration. He peered intently at a seemingly random pattern of thin swirling lines of many different colours, talking to himself quietly in his reedy voice. 'Where are you hiding, you ***traitor?*** You can't tuck yourself away within the timelines forever, you know. Sooner or later, I will find you. Oh yes, my friend, I will find you.'

(Doctor Proteus is a fairly creepy character, just in case that's not coming across.)

A-Z
A-Z
A-Z

Suddenly, a gigantic shadow blocked the doorway behind him and a deep, rumbling voice spoke out of the darkness: 'Have you located the ***runaway?***'

Proteus cringed. 'Not yet, my lord. But it's only a matter of time.' A slow, gloating smile spread across his thin lips and he cracked his knuckles. 'She cannot hide forever.'

CHAPTER 6

THE SUNKEN CITY

You may well be wondering, what does travelling through time in a shopping trolley with a wonky wheel feel like? After all, it's probably not something that many of us are going to experience – like being the US president, or unexpectedly becoming a cow. Well, travelling through time in a wonky-wheeled trolley feels a lot like going on a roller coaster. Only a really, really big one. In a shopping trolley. In other words, it's ***very fast*** and it makes you feel like your stomach has travelled through your body and is trying to squeeze its way out through your ears. (Bet you're quite glad you're not going to experience it now, aren't you?)

Angus hadn't been quite prepared for his first trip

through time. After all, he'd just fallen backwards into a shopping trolley holding a dog, and that had taken a lot of his attention. This time he was ready. But he wasn't fully prepared for what happened after the Time Trolley disappeared from the car park of Hyper-Buy. As before, it headed into the blue and purple of what Marge had described as the chill-out zone. But this time, instead of floating calmly through the swirling light and the plinky-plunky whale music, it ***lurched sickeningly*** from side to side, bucking up and down like a cross horse.

'What's . . . going . . . on?' Angus managed to blurt in between swerves. Peering out through the metal mesh, he could see the colours swirling faster and in more random, strange patterns than before. McQueen whimpered in alarm and pawed at the sides of the trolley.

'I don't know,' shouted Marge. 'Hattie? Hattie? What's going on?'

'**I was about to ask you the same question**,' replied Hattie. '**We didn't launch in a straight line. That wheel seems to have messed up the time fix.**'

'Told you these things never steer straight,' said Angus through gritted teeth.

'**Hold on,**' said Hattie's voice. '**I think I've managed to stabilize the time trajectory. Anyway, we're coming in to land somewhere. *Buckle up*.**'

Angus groped behind him to try and fasten his seatbelt but found there wasn't one.

'***HOW AM I SUPPOSED TO BUCKLE UP?***'

he shouted, as the trolley plunged downwards through the void.

'**It's just an expression,**' Hattie told him calmly. '**Early twenty-first-century slang. I thought you'd be familiar with it.**'

Angus was about to say something rude, but he was stopped by a blaze of blinding sunlight and a wash of heat on his face. Before he closed his eyes against the glare he caught a glimpse of sand dunes, shimmering in a baking haze of heat and coming rapidly closer. Seconds later he was treated to an entire mouthful of sand as the trolley planted itself in a large dune, slowly toppled over on its side and spilled them out in the hot desert.

'**Certainly looks a lot like Ancient Egypt to me,**' Hattie went on. '**Hang on, just computing. I'll find out where we are.**' Angus rolled over and picked up McQueen, using his other hand to shield his eyes. '**Yes, it's Egypt all right,**' the computer continued. '**Nile Delta, 342 BC. We're just outside the city of Thonis. Only a few hundred years outside the target range. Just call me the master of wonky-wheel control . . . or M.W.W.C. for short if you prefer.**'

'Fourth century BC?' said Marge, sounding grumpy as she got to her feet and shook some sand out of her waistcoat pockets. 'That's not where we were supposed to be at all! There might not even be any ***cheese*** here!'

'**You're welcome,**' said Hattie quietly and huffily.

'And we're too far north as well,' grumbled Marge, ignoring this digital sarcasm. 'I was going to show him those pyramids they're always going on about.' She finished dusting herself down. 'Come on, history boy. Let's find some stuff for your project and get ourselves out of here. Don't forget to keep that on!' She pointed to the earpiece in his ear. 'Right, I think we're ready,' she said decisively. 'Hattie, how long have we got?'

'**Calculating battery reserves,**' replied the computer. '**OK – timing return jump in sixty minutes. Repeat, you have exactly one hour. Coordinates locked for our return to the A.I. period. So hurry up and do your funky Ancient Egyptian thing. Don't be late, cos I won't wait!**'

'Why have we only got an hour?' Angus complained, wondering briefly what the A.I. period might be. 'I thought we could hang out here for a bit, you know . . . and grab some Ancient Egyptian food? Talk to a few people and get this presentation done?'

'The Time Trolley's ***electric***,' Marge explained. 'If we stay here too long, Hattie's battery will run down. And if that happens, we've got two options. First, we can get her up to eight miles per hour to power the trolley. And good luck trying that by rolling down a sand dune.' She gestured out across the desert. 'In fact, it's really difficult getting a shopping trolley up to eight miles per hour

anywhere in ancient history. Even those Roman roads aren't really smooth enough. And they're always too flat.'

'OK,' said Angus, trudging after her in his increasingly sand-filled trainers. 'So you can't roll the trolley downhill to power it up. But you said there are two options. What's plan B?'

'Oh,' Marge replied. 'We just wait around until someone discovers ***electricity***, then plug her into the wall.'

'**And that is over two thousand years away,**' added Hattie's voice inside Angus's head. '**So I strongly suggest you're back in the trolley on time. Because the return jump is now locked in. I'm leaving on time – with you or without you.**'

'Besides,' said Marge, 'I'd better take this thing back and have a look at that wheel. Can't be zipping all over time like a jack-in-the-box. Who knows where I might end up? And keep a close hold on that dog!' She was now nearing the top of the dune and Angus, with McQueen tucked safely under his arm, followed on behind. When they finally reached the top, he gasped in amazement. Spread out below them, dazzling in the clear sunlit air, was the lost, ancient city of Thonis.

FACT PIG

HI, KIDS! It's the Fact Pig here, with some fun facts for you! That's right, guys! History is super exciting! **Oink!** Listen to this! Thonis-Heracleion was a major port and trading centre. It was built across a network of canals, just like Venice! **Snort!** It was Ancient Egypt's bustling gateway to the Mediterranean! But it has now completely disappeared beneath the sea. Archaeologists have found the remains of the city underwater! Wow! Isn't that exciting?

SHUT UP*, *Fact Pig, this isn't a history lesson. Let us get on with the story.

But I was going to tell them about the huge temple in the city, dedicated to the god Amun!

No, be quiet. Here, shut up and have a banana.

But I'm a pig. I don't eat bananas.

Well, just shut up, then. We're carrying on with the story.

Angus and Marge slid down the other side of the dune, heading for the outskirts of the city not far away. And, without getting all Fact Piggy about it, it really did look ***incredible***. Thonis was built beside a wide, slow-moving river dotted with boats. A single wide bridge crossed the river towards the city itself, which was built on a network of islands. Between them, wooden bridges criss-crossed canals, and in between the dazzling waterways, elaborate buildings of brightly painted stone clustered together. More of the tall-masted boats were anchored at the busy wharves, and the streets were crowded with people going about their business or stopping to chat in the patches of shade. As the time travellers approached, the warm breeze carried the scent of spices and the aroma of frying fish towards them.

'This,' said Angus breathlessly as he tagged along beside Marge, crossing the wide wooden bridge and heading into town, 'is brilliant!' His eye was caught by a disturbance in the brownish river, and he was startled to see a ***large crocodile*** swim beneath them, its scaly back sticking out of the water and its tail moving in a lazy corkscrew motion.

'Hmm,' said Marge. 'It's all right, I suppose, if you like that kind of thing. Wait till you try the cheese, though. You won't be so excited then.'

On the far side of the bridge was a large area paved with stone, near a series of wooden docks where the ships were tied up. Several small stalls had been set up where people were shopping or bartering. At the wharf, men and women were loading and unloading boxes and bags of cargo from the ships, using wooden cranes hung with heavy weights or simply passing bales of cloth or bags of goods from hand to hand. Plenty of other townsfolk were clustered round, talking, laughing, munching on snacks from some of the wooden stands or simply watching what was going on. Angus and Marge stopped too, squinting up at the masts against the blue sky. And Angus, despite having little interest in history on the page of a book, felt that he could have simply stopped and stared at this actual, living piece of history forever.

'Aren't you ***hot*** in that?' said a voice at Angus's side, and a hand plucked at the sleeve of his sweatshirt.

'**Translating from Egyptian, northern coastal dialect, middle kingdom,**' said Hattie in his ear. '**And I'll translate**

For you too – or to put it another way . . . you can now talk like an Egyptian. *Get it?* Oh, never mind.'

Angus turned to see who had spoken to him. There, standing beside him and looking him curiously up and down, was a girl about his own age. She was dressed in a simple white tunic, with gold bangles on her wrists. Her head was shaved apart from one thick braid on the left-hand side and her eyes were lined with the black make-up he recognized from his history textbook.

'I said, aren't you hot?' the girl repeated, tugging once again on the thick material of his sleeve. 'Was it cold where you sailed from?'

'***Erm***,' said Angus intelligently. It's not the most sizzling thing to say to the first ever Ancient Egyptian you meet, but give him a break. He's just travelled more than two thousand years – which is even more time than it takes to drive to Cornwall on a Friday.

'Yes,' he continued honestly. 'I am kind of hot, actually.' As he spoke, he was once again aware that different sounds were coming out of his mouth. But, surprisingly, he was already getting used to Hattie's incredible translation abilities. The fact that he was speaking to a real-life Ancient Egyptian was too exciting to freak out about a computer messing with your brainwaves.

'Hello, dear,' said Marge, coming over and holding out her paper bag. 'Do you want a ***jelly baby?*** ' The girl took one suspiciously and sniffed at it. 'Do you know where the market is?' Marge went on kindly. 'May as well pick up some cheese while we're here, I suppose,' she added out of the corner of her mouth to Angus. 'Even if it is completely revolting.'

'Oh, and I also want to find out what daily life was – sorry, is – like in Ancient Egypt,' added Angus, remembering his homework.

'***Ancient?***' said the girl, frowning.

'Sorry,' said Angus again. 'I meant, present-day Egypt. Obviously. You were right,' he added to Marge, 'this does take quite a lot of getting used to.'

CHAPTER 7

THE OLDEST CHEESE IN THE WORLD

'Mmmm.' The girl was examining him curiously. 'You're really not from round here, are you?' she asked. 'Your garments are ***very strange***. But we see a lot of travellers in Thonis. Come on,' she beckoned and led them towards a side street. 'Market's this way. My name's Akila, by the way. A-KEE-LA,' she repeated, seeing Angus frowning. 'And you are?'

'I'm Marge,' said Marge as they followed. 'And this is Angus.'

'***AN-GHOOS?***' repeated Akila. 'That's a weird noise, isn't it? Is that a common name in the cold place you sailed from?' She seemed convinced they'd arrived on one of the boats at the dock, and Angus decided this made an excellent cover story.

'That's right,' he said confidently. 'Loads of An-ghooses where I come from. Pleased to meet you. And this is McQueen, by the way,' he added, nodding towards the dog. Akila, apparently noticing him for the first time, started back in surprise. 'Don't see many of those,' she told him. 'What's he for? ***Hunting?***'

'Well, he sometimes hunts through the kitchen bin,' said Angus. 'Unless my mum catches him first.'

'I think Ancient Egyptians are more cat people,' Hattie's voice told him inside his head. Akila, with another questioning look at them both, continued leading them through the bustling streets of the city. Eventually they came to an open space where several traders had laid out produce on woven mats on the stone paving. 'That's the cheese guy, over there,' said the Egyptian girl, pointing to a mat where a large man had placed a series of wicker baskets in the shade.

'Good afternoon, my friends!' he said as they approached. 'You're strangely dressed – just off the boat? No matter, no matter.' Angus realized that, being a busy port, they must be used to seeing different outfits here. 'Would you like some of this fine cheese?' the stallholder went on. 'Very fresh, very delicious.'

'So, where did you sail from?' asked Akila, placing her hands on her hips and facing Angus. Behind her, Marge was negotiating a price for one of his cheeses.

'Oh, I don't think you'll have heard of it,' Angus said, panicking slightly as he remembered that Marge had warned him not to draw too much attention to himself. 'It's a very faraway place. I mean, literally ages away.'

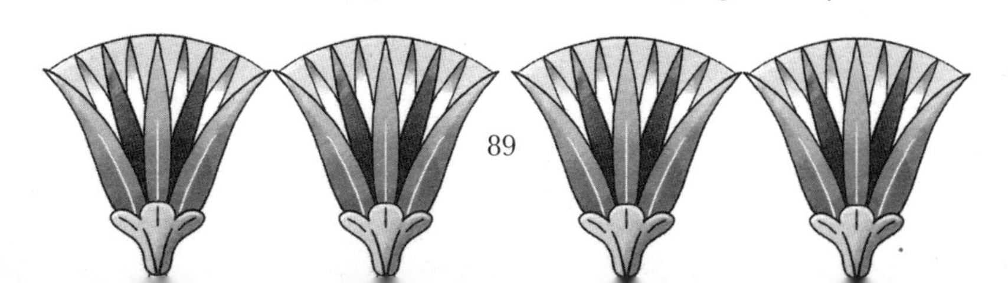

'I bet I would have heard of it,' countered Akila, looking him in the eye curiously. 'My father's a merchant. He sails all over the place, and he always brings stories back from the lands he visits. I love hearing stories about different places. What's your story?'

Angus decided that this curious girl was getting far too interested in where he came from. 'Seriously,' he said, 'you wouldn't have heard of it. It's the faraway land of, erm –' he thought frantically – '**car park!**' he blurted out finally, remembering the place they had, in fact, recently travelled from.

Akila tipped her head to one side quizzically. 'Karp Arkh?' she asked him. 'I actually don't think I've heard of that place. Is it somewhere beyond Phoenicia? You must have had a long voyage.'

'Oh, really, really long,' agreed Angus. 'Took us absolutely centuries.' Behind him, he could vaguely hear Marge concluding her cheese deal.

'What's life like in Karp Arkh, then?' Akila wanted to know, reaching out and grabbing his arm in a friendly manner. 'Come on, you must have some amazing stories. What's good to eat there? What gods do you worship? Is there a big temple?'

'Well, there's a new shopping centre on the bypass,' began Angus uneasily. But before he could go on he was interrupted by Marge, who had turned away from the stall.

'Here we are, then,' she said triumphantly. 'You said you wanted to have some Ancient Egyptian food. Voilà! Ancient cheese! Just about the oldest cheese on the planet, if you're interested. Want a taste?' She was holding out one of the clay pots and brandishing a small wooden spoon in her other hand.

From a young age, Angus's parents had encouraged him to try a lot of different foods. They hadn't wanted him to grow up to be a fussy eater. So he took the spoon Marge was proffering and dipped it slightly suspiciously into the pot. The substance inside wasn't much like what we think of as cheese. It was yellowish and quite liquid, with smallish ***lumps*** in it. And, as Angus brought the spoon close to his mouth, he also realized that it smelled more than a little bad. Imagine if you locked nine goats in a room and made them ride exercise bikes for four hours straight without opening the windows. Kind of like that. *Still,* he thought to himself, remembering what his dad once told him about Brussels sprouts, *you can't say you don't like something unless you've tasted it.* And he put the spoon in his mouth.

'BLAAARGGGGGHHHH!'

Angus felt as if an entire layer of his tongue had been stripped off. 'That is revolting!' he said, giving a large and very reluctant swallow.

'Oi!' complained the stallholder. 'That's the best camel cheese in all of Thonis!'

'Camel cheese?' echoed Angus. 'Gah!'

'He's not local,' explained Akila to the stallholder in a mollifying tone. 'He's from the city of Karp Arkh.'

'Told you the cheese here is disgusting,' said Marge, sounding satisfied. 'We should have gone to Renaissance Italy for the really good stuff. Hey –' she suddenly broke off – 'I thought I told you to keep an eye on that dog!'

Angus looked round in shock. Sure enough, McQueen's fluffy brown tail was just disappearing down a narrow side alley. Distracted by the mouthful of camel cheese, he'd unthinkingly let him go. 'McQueen!' he shouted desperately. 'Here, boy! Come back!' The only reply was a delighted bark that echoed back around the courtyard. McQueen, who'd spotted a cat slinking away through the streets, had no intention of coming back. He was having the time of his life.

'**Temporal resolve in twenty minutes,**' said the voice of Hattie the computer, unhelpfully. '***Hurry back***, **people. Battery level's getting low. Time to go home.**'

'You have got to be joking,' said Marge tersely. 'Come on, quick! We must find that dog and get back to the time machine.'

'Do you want some help?' asked Akila.

'Yes, please.' Angus turned to her gratefully. 'Do you think you could help me find my dog? We're in a bit of a hurry. Our time machine . . . I mean, sorry, our *ship* is, er, setting sail really soon. And we need to be on it.'

'I'll help you, on one condition,' said Akila, again giving him that keen, curious look.

'Anything. Yes. What?'

'You have to tell me all about ***where you're from***,' she said, narrowing her black-rimmed eyes. 'Where you're *really* from,' she added with a smile. 'I bet your dog's doubled back towards the wharves,' she added. 'I'll go and check over there and I'll meet you back by your ship.' She turned and began to weave her way through the crowds back towards the river.

'How will you find us?' Angus shouted after her.

'You won't be difficult to track down,' she yelled over her shoulder. 'Not in those hot clothes!'

'Too curious by far, that one,' said Marge, peering suspiciously after Akila as she left the square and disappeared into an alleyway. 'Right, let's find that runaway dog – ***quickly!*** I knew it was a bad idea to bring a dog to ancient history,' she went on in an angry mutter as they raced off in pursuit. 'People find it hard to keep control of them round the supermarket, let alone in an ancient city where they literally worship cats.'

'Excuse me, please,' shouted Angus, feeling the unfamiliar words coming out of his mouth as Hattie interpreted for him. The crowd of Egyptians parted for him, and a group of curious children, their heads shaved and with a single braid just like Akila's, began to follow him as he raced away in the direction where McQueen had disappeared. As he crossed a short bridge over a narrow canal he thought he could hear the distant sound of pattering paws, so they chased it down a small side street. The street turned first to the left, then the right, but they were clearly going the right way. Now and then an ***excited bark*** echoed back from the stone walls on either side and once or twice Angus even caught a brief glimpse of a furry brown shape as he ran. Eventually, a large archway appeared at the end of the street and they quickened their pace towards it. Bursting through the arch, Angus had to shield his eyes against the sunlight once again. After the shade of the alleyways, the glare was dazzling.

He and Marge had blundered into an enormous open space, apparently right in the middle of the city. To one side of them rose a gigantic temple, with huge steps leading up to a wide portico with tall painted statues of various gods standing on stout plinths. A group of people in richly embroidered robes were processing slowly up the steps, chanting, as the crowds beneath parted respectfully to let them through.

'Looks like it's time for church,' said Marge brightly. 'Oh, look, there's your dog. **Quick!**' She pointed. Sure enough, McQueen was visible at one side of the crowd, sitting down politely on his haunches to watch the priests file past. The cat he'd been chasing could be seen slipping smugly inside the temple with a whisk of its tail.

'**Got you!**' As Angus scooped up his dog, he took a moment to examine the gigantic statues on his left. One god had the head of a crocodile, another looked like a thickly muscled man with the head and torso of a bull. He'd seen similar things in his textbook – photographs of statues that had been dug up by archaeologists.

But instead of the sandy-coloured stone he was used to, these were painted in vivid reds and blues, with chunky golden jewellery around their necks, woven scarves draped around their shoulders and thick carpets of flowers laid at their feet. There was no more time for sightseeing, though.

'Temporal resolve in ten minutes,' declared Hattie, and Marge clutched her head in alarm.

'We're going to have to ***really shift***,' she said. 'Come on!' And, with Angus clutching McQueen even more tightly this time, they tore out of the square and off towards the sand dunes visible beyond the edge of the city. They thudded over more wooden bridges and raced through streets crowded with people looking to Angus as if they were on their way to a fancy-dress party. Except, of course, they weren't. The only people in fancy dress were Angus and Marge.

'Time travel really involves a lot of running about, doesn't it?' Angus panted as they finally reached the wharf where they'd first run into Akila. He looked from side to side but was disappointed to discover that the girl was nowhere to be seen. She'd been bright and curious, and he realized he'd been looking forward to chatting to her again, even if only briefly.

'It doesn't usually involve this much running, to be honest,' replied Marge, who had gone rather red in the face. 'I usually just pick up some cheese for the counter, have a bit of a natter and head home again. You're making it much more dramatic than most of my trips, what with accidental jewel theft and runaway dogs. You're a time-travelling liability, you are. Good job this is your last trip.' And once again Angus felt that tug of disappointment in his midriff. He realized he didn't want this to be his last visit to history. In real life it was far, far more interesting and exciting than his lessons had led him to believe. Even taking the ***revolting*** cheese into account.

'**Temporal resolve in three minutes, guys. That's three minutes. Not five, not four. Actually three,**' said Hattie as they thundered across the main bridge out of Thonis and began the knee-punishing climb up the high dune on the other side. Her computerized voice sounded slightly less calm than usual. '**And I really do suggest you get a move on. Bit of a *situation* here.**'

'Situation?' questioned Marge.

'What happens if we don't make it in time?' Angus puffed at the same time. 'Will one of your time-travelling friends come and get us?'

'I don't have any time-travelling friends,' she told him. 'There's just me. If the trolley goes back without us, well . . . you'd better get used to Egyptian food, basically.

And get yourself a nice head shave like that girl you took a shine to.' Angus was too exhausted to respond to this. It's incredibly difficult to run up a sand dune, and the added pressure of being trapped thousands of years in the past wasn't making things any less tense and sweaty. Finally they reached the crest of the dune and ***flung*** themselves towards the Time Trolley, which was standing neatly halfway down the slope. Everything was starting to look more positive, apart from one slightly tricky detail.

This was the tricky detail: the Ancient Egyptian girl Akila was sitting in the trolley.

The trolley that was about to catapult itself back to our own time in approximately eighty-three seconds.

Tricky, right?

'Is this your chariot?' she called as Marge and Angus barrelled down the slope towards her, waving their arms. 'It's really odd-shaped. Where do you attach the horse?'

'What are you doing in there?' cried Marge.

'I told you I was going to find out where you came from,' replied Akila. 'I like meeting travellers and hearing their tales. Someone at the wharf said you came from this direction, so I followed your footprints.'

'**Temporal resolve imminent,**' said Hattie. '**Get in! Now!**'

'We need to get her out first!' said Marge shrilly.

'**There isn't time!**' the computer told her. '**Five, four . . .**'

'**Warrgh!**'

said Marge, leaping into the trolley.

'**Flaargh!**'

added Angus as he did the same.

'Are we going for a chariot ride?' asked Akila.

'Erm –' Angus searched for a way to explain this to her and completely failed to find one. 'Kind of? Hang on tight.'

'Why is your chariot ***glowing?***'

'**Three . . . two . . .**'

'Oh, great,' Marge sighed. 'Another unwanted passenger.'

'**One.**'

And with a flash and a snap, the Time Trolley vanished from the desert, startling several nearby camels.

CHAPTER 8

THE WONKY WHEEL

If the Time Trolley had behaved oddly on their way to Ancient Egypt, that was ***nothing*** compared to what happened when they tried to go home again. A stream of bright sparks was shooting out of one of the front wheels – and instead of veering from side to side, the trolley started spinning sickeningly. Instead of the calming blue and purple of the chill-out zone, it now appeared to be racing through nothing but inky blackness.

MEANWHEN IN THE FAR FUTURE . . .

'Aha!' Doctor Proteus jabbed a bony finger at the interweaving coloured lines on his screen. 'A disturbance in the timeline! This must be it!' With his other hand he tapped feverishly at his computer keys. 'If I can just narrow it down to this one stream, I can find her hiding place,' he said to himself. 'And then I will be able to plant the virus,' he went on, licking his lips hungrily. 'I shall bring the time device to my master. And then, at last . . . he will be ***unstoppable***.' He followed this, as you might expect, with an evil cackle.

'Why are you emitting an ***evil cackle?***' said a deep voice from behind him. 'Have you located the fugitive?'

'I believe I may have, Your Foulness,' said Proteus, his bloodshot eyes flicking nervously to one side. 'I just need to follow this trail through history, but we are close. Very, very close.'

'Excellent,' gloated the voice from behind him. 'Truly excellent. Soon we shall locate her. And then, finally . . . I shall have my revenge.'

BACK IN THE TROLLEY . . .

'What on earth is going on?' yelled Marge as the three of them clutched the metal sides tightly.

'***Graaaargh!***' shrieked Akila, her eyes wide with alarm. 'What? Whatwhatwhat? ***Fleeergh!*** What's going ON?! Where are we? What happened? What kind of chariot is this? I thought you said you came on a ship? How do I get home?'

'**Can we perhaps deal with those questions one at a time?**' asked Hattie calmly.

'Who said THAT?!' shrieked Akila. 'Am I dead? Is this Duat?'

FACT PIG

HI, KIDS! FACT PIG HERE!

Oh, flipping heck.

Duat is the Ancient Egyptian underworld. They believed that when you die –

SHUT UP*, *Fact Pig. They can look this stuff up for themselves. This is an adventure story. Stop trying to educate people.

'What we're looking at here, boys and girls,' said the computerized voice of Hattie, **'is a *full-on guidance system malfunction*. Looks like that wonky wheel at the front has sent my whole time-lock matrix out of sync.'** The trolley continued to spin dizzyingly, plunging up and down like a small boat on a choppy sea.

'I think I might pass out,' said Akila faintly, her braid whipping from side to side as the trolley lurched.

'All things considered, dear, I think that might be an excellent idea,' said Marge kindly.

'So, Hattie,' asked Angus, 'guidance system malfunction. What does that mean, exactly?'

'It means,' said Hattie, **'that we could end up *absolutely anywhere*. Or, to be exact, anywhere and any*when*.'**

'Is *anywhen* actually a word?' asked Marge.

'You're in a shopping trolley hurtling through time and you're concerned about grammar?' retorted Hattie. **'And yes, actually it is a word.'**

'What in the name of Horus, Anubis, Osiris and Ra is going on?' said Akila faintly. 'I don't understand what any of you are talking about!'

'I did warn you it's complicated,' Angus told her, with a comforting pat on her shoulder. 'Don't worry, we'll get you home.' Privately, he very much hoped that was true. He wasn't even sure if he was going to get back to his own time, but this seemed like a bad moment to panic.

'**Hold on,**' said Hattie. '**It looks like we're about to touch down somewhen.**'

'Somewhen?' questioned Marge. But before they could repeat the previous grammar argument, there was a thud and a flash of light, and the trolley pitched forward, throwing them out on to a patch of damp, muddy ground. The air was warm and humid, and tall ferns waved all around.

'**Another *happy landing*,**' said Hattie in a satisfied tone.

'When are we?' asked Marge, looking around nervously. 'Doesn't look like any part of history I recognize. Bet there isn't even a cheese shop. Anyway,' she said to Akila, 'while we've got a couple of minutes, I can probably answer your questions. I daresay you've got a few.'

'Try not to freak out,' Angus warned her, and Akila gave a shaky nod.

'So, to summarize,' Marge continued, 'you climbed into our chariot and you've accidentally come with us on our journey. This is a bit of a ***special*** chariot, though –'

'Because it can travel to different parts of time?' Akila broke in. Marge looked startled.

'Well, yes,' she replied. 'How did you work that out?'

'You said it, when we were spinning around in that weird black place,' Akila pointed out. 'I told you, I like listening to people's stories. I pay attention, that's all.'

'Well, I must say, you're taking it a lot more calmly than young Angus here!' Marge congratulated her, offering her another jelly baby. Sure enough, Angus was darting from one side of the shopping trolley to the other, casting nervous glances into the undergrowth. 'What's the matter with you?' Marge asked him. 'Prehistoric ants in your pants?'

'Hattie,' said Angus, ignoring her, 'have you calculated exactly when we are yet?'

'Will you be able to take me home?' Akila asked Marge.

'Oh, yes,' Marge reassured her. 'As soon as I get that wheel fixed, I'll have you back in Ancient Egypt in no time at all. I can drop you off right after we met you. No problem.'

'In that case,' said Akila, 'I'm going to find out as much as I can about the strange places we travel to. Not many people get the chance to go on such an exciting journey, right?'

'Right, dear,' said Marge, looking very impressed at her composure.

Angus was now pointing with a trembling finger at the mud just outside the trolley. Something had caught his eye – a large, three-toed footprint with ***claw marks*** clearly visible in front of it.

'I really, really hope that isn't what I think it is,' he said out loud.

'**Why?**' asked Hattie. '**What do you think it is?**'

'I think . . .' Angus looked around the clearing nervously. 'I think it's a footprint. To be exact, the footprint of a d–'

At that point, he was interrupted by a loud, hoarse ***wailing*** from somewhere off in the trees. '**I think you might want to prepare yourselves,**' Hattie told them. '**We appear to have shot quite a long way backwards through the time field. Quite a few million years, in fact.**'

There was a rustling from somewhere away to the right. 'Are we, by any chance, in the Jurassic era?' asked Angus, scuttling backwards towards the trolley and standing next to Marge and Akila.

'Jurassic era?' said Akila, looking interested. 'That's a funny word. What does it mean?'

'**Jurassic era, that's right,**' said Hattie. '**How did you know?**'

'Oh, you know,' said Angus airily. 'I just thought what the ***worst possible situation*** could be and assumed that was what had happened.' Once again, the piercing, roaring noise rose from the forest.

Akila was looking around curiously at the tall ferns. 'That mountain over there's on fire,' she said, pointing. Sure enough, on the horizon was a large volcano, smoking ominously.

'Ooh,' said Marge. 'Well spotted. Very interesting.'

'That's how it starts,' said Angus tersely. 'Ooh, a volcano. But then later, there's running and ***screaming***.'

'Why are you being so weird?' Akila wanted to know. 'If anybody should be panicking at this point, it should be me.'

'She's right, you know,' agreed Marge. 'Why don't you

take a papyrus leaf out of Akila's book? Panicking never helped anyone, you know.'

'You wouldn't say that if you'd seen the films I've seen,' replied Angus, as once again a roaring howl echoed from the faraway mountains. 'Can you identify that animal noise, please, Hattie?' he asked.

'**Computing that,**' replied the computer. '**Stand by.**'

'What do you mean, stand by?' asked Marge. 'You're the ***most powerful computer ever invented***. You don't need thinking time!'

'**I just thought it would build the tension,**' Hattie replied casually. '**All right, then, Mrs Impatient. If you're so keen to have the answer straight away – that is the cry of a velociraptor.**' At this point, Angus decided that time travel really, really wasn't his cup of tea. There was another rustle in the bushes off to the right, and Marge turned to face it.

'Don't you know anything about velociraptors?' asked Angus, rapidly turning in a circle to keep his eyes on the whole clearing. 'That rustling over there is just a distraction. The other raptors are somewhere behind us. Then, when we're distracted by the rustling, they all leap out and we say "***clever girl***" and then they eat us.'

'What are you gabbling about?' asked Akila.

'Velociraptors are bad news,' babbled Angus. 'They leap out and slash at us with their long claws. Which would really, really hurt. Can we go, please?'

'**Guidance system's still offline,**' Hattie told him. '**Give me a minute. Try not to get eaten in the meantime.**'

'We're being hunted,' wailed Angus, shrinking back against the trolley and sinking to his knees.

At that point, the rustling in the ferns became even louder. And, as Angus gave a startled wail of '***Don't move!*** It can't see us if we don't move!' a creature leapt out from the undergrowth and stood facing them. Well, we say 'leapt' – it was more of a hop, to be honest. The dinosaur didn't look much like a dinosaur. At least, not the kind that Angus had read about in books or seen in the cinema. It looked much more like a turkey, with brownish feathers covering its body and a long, beak-like face. It was about the size of a turkey, as well. In other words, not particularly terrifying.

'What is *that*?' said Angus.

'**Oh, that?**' came Hattie's reply. '**That's a velociraptor.**'

'No, it isn't,' said Angus. 'It looks like a slightly oversized chicken.' The velociraptor gave a small gobbling noise and looked at them curiously, its feathery head tilted to one side.

'How do you know all this?' asked Akila, looking at him quizzically.

'Oh, just from . . . dinosaur books,' Angus told her. 'They're basically the only ones I liked reading at primary school.'

'What's a ***dinosaur?***' Akila asked. 'And what's a book? And what's a primary school?' At this point, Angus realized that the explanation he was going to have to deliver to the Ancient Egyptian girl was going to take rather a long time.

FACT PIG

Hi again, kids! It's the **Fact Pig** again, with some incredible piggy facts about dinosaurs! **Wow!** Contrary to popular belief, velociraptors were only actually the size of turkeys.

SHUT UP*, *Fact Pig, we've already made that quite obvious in the actual story. Stop interrupting.

And did you know that the word **'dinosaur'** actually means 'terrible lizard'?

YES, we did, everybody knows that. Back in your box.

Bye for now, kids! More cool history **FACTS** coming up soon! **Oink!**

'I think you've been watching too many films,' said Marge. 'Haven't you learned yet? History's almost never what you expect it to be. And it's far more interesting than those lessons would have you believe.' At this point, McQueen, who had been cowering inside the trolley, leapt out and barked frantically at the dinosaur, which took to its heels with a startled squawk and vanished back into the forest. The little dog looked back at Angus with a proud expression that said: 'I've just seen off an ***actual velociraptor***. If that doesn't deserve a treat, I don't know what does.'

'**Back in the trolley,**' Hattie told them. '**We're ready for take-off. Hopefully I can get us home this time.**' But she was wrong. With a flash, the trolley vanished from the prehistoric jungle, then began to spin crazily through time, sparks shooting from the wonky front wheel.

Once again, they landed with a *thump* somewhere very unexpected.

This time, they found themselves in a neat and tidy front garden. Flower beds surrounded a tidy lawn with

a white-painted wooden fence, and, in front of them was a spic-and-span thatched cottage.

'**Stratford-upon-Avon, AD 1589,**' Hattie told them. '**If you had any English lit homework, now would be the perfect time. My records show that this house belongs to a Mr William Shakespeare.**'

'He was a really famous playwright,' Angus told Akila.

'Ah,' she responded. 'We actually have those at home. But it's ***cold*** here, isn't it?' She gave a small shiver. To be fair, it was a chilly day in Stratford-upon-Avon. Chillier than back in Thonis, anyway. Suddenly, the front door of the cottage was pulled open to reveal a tall, cross-looking woman in a dark dress.

'***What are you doing in my rosemary bush?***' she shrieked at them.

'Oh, hello, Anne,' said Marge smoothly. 'Is Will at home?'

'*I've met him a few times,*' she explained in an undertone to Angus. '*Gave him a couple of nice ideas about cheese to put in his little plays.*'

'No, he's not at home! And who wants to know?! He's never at bloomin' home!' replied the woman in the

doorway. 'He's off in London, gallivanting around with a load of red-tighted show-offs. An' I'm here, up to me eyes in it! Both kids down with the bloomin' plague, I've run out of leeches and I've got more housework than you can ***shake a spear*** at.'

'Sorry, did Shakespeare's wife just do a . . . Shakespeare pun?' enquired Angus, open-mouthed. But as Marge was about to answer, the trolley began shaking violently and with a jolt and a jerk, they disappeared again into the blackness.

'Typical,' said Anne Hathaway, tutting and rolling her eyes. 'And just when I could have done with a hand turning the mattress over on the second-best bed.'

Authors' Note:

We have inserted this Shakespeare joke in a pathetic attempt to get this book on the ***Key Stage 2 curriculum***. Well, it's got to be worth a shot, right? In Shakespeare's will, he left his wife the ***second-best bed***. Isn't that a fascinating fact? Gah! We're turning into the Fact Pig. On with the story.

Once again, Angus held on for dear life as the Time Trolley pinballed crazily through the ***nothingness*** of the time void. Akila held on tight to the back of his sweatshirt, uttering the occasional squeak of alarm. 'Status update, Hattie?' said Marge through gritted teeth as the trolley took another alarming lurch that nearly spilled them all out sideways.

'**Think I've almost got it,**' replied the calm voice.

'You think? Almost?' Marge's voice rose to a panicked shriek. 'For a hugely advanced computer from the ninety-ninth century you're not very exact, are you?'

'The ***ninety-ninth*** century?' Angus's mouth fell open.

'You weren't supposed to hear that! Forget I spoke!' Marge, for the first time, had started to look properly flustered. The trolley had righted itself but was still racing along so uncertainly that, at times, it was hard to tell whether they were shooting forward or backwards. Abruptly, it gave the biggest lurch yet, like a horse that's decided it's done with being ridden all the flipping time, and plunged downwards.

'**This feels just about right,**' said Hattie's voice inside Angus's head. '**I reckon we're heading back towards the A.I. period. Hold on tight, time pirates!**'

'Time pirates?' Marge looked confused.

'**My systems tell me that giving something a *cool title* makes it much less alarming,**' the computer replied. '**I calculated that if I refer to these young humans as "time pirates", it should distract them from the possibility that they are about to be *ripped***

apart **by the conflicting timelines, meaning their entire existence will be permanently erased.**'

'***WHAT?***' Angus did not like the idea of his entire existence being permanently erased. Well, to be fair, it does sound kind of alarming.

'**I should not have said that out loud,**' Hattie replied. '**Don't worry – hey, you're a *time pirate!***'

'That's not going to work *now*, is it?' bellowed Angus, catching Akila's eye and giving her what he hoped was a reassuring expression. In fact, it looked as if he'd just swallowed a giant bee, but at least he'd tried.

The trolley continued to plunge downwards, sparks still shooting from the front wheel. And now, bolts of thin electricity began to fizz up and down the metal framework. The sides of the trolley became warm to the touch, then so hot that some sections actually began to glow red. Marge, Angus and Akila huddled in the centre, trying not to touch the burning metal, although sometimes it was impossible as the trolley swerved left and right. Suddenly, there was a gigantic flash of white light and the trolley tipped over, spilling them out once again on to the ground.

Angus rolled over several times before he came to a halt and cautiously opened his eyes to find he was lying on cold, damp concrete.

'I don't think I've ever been so glad to see a patch of concrete,' he said shakily, rolling over again and looking up at the familiar orange street light above him. A quick glance to his left confirmed that they had, indeed, landed back in the car park of Hyper-Buy. 'And I don't think I've ever been ***so relieved*** to see the doors of a supermarket,' he added.

'What about when you really, really need to buy toilet paper?' countered Marge, who was getting to her feet nearby and rushing to help Akila, who had tumbled out first. Angus, still wobbly-legged with adrenaline, staggered over to join them.

'**If anybody wanted to give me a round of applause,**' said Hattie smugly, '**this would be the perfect moment. Without my guidance systems being fully online, I have landed us right back where we first picked Angus up, in his home period of A.I. And the award for "most awesome time navigation computer" goes to: *ME!* You're welcome.**'

'Why did you say you'd come from the ninety-ninth century?' asked Angus accusingly as he approached Marge. The cheese salesperson had lifted Akila gently to her feet and placed a comforting arm around her shoulders. The girl was shivering and looking around the supermarket car park with a fearful expression.

'No time for all that now!' Marge said, shushing him with an upraised finger. 'We need to take care of this one. She's in danger of going into time-shock. She needs warming up. And a chunk of **good Cheddar**, I shouldn't wonder.'

'It really is all about cheese with you, isn't it?'

'Grab the trolley,' Marge instructed him, 'and follow me.' Angus righted the Time Trolley, which still had smoke pouring from the front left-hand wheel, and steered it back up towards the top of the car park. Marge led him to a side-door at the right of the main sliding doors to the shop floor. Unlocking this, she ushered Akila through, and Angus followed them, pushing the trolley with McQueen riding inside.

They entered a small storeroom, with cardboard boxes stacked high up each of the walls. A few plastic chairs were scattered about, and Marge led Akila to one of these before busying herself at a trestle table where a kettle stood behind a selection of mugs, jars and boxes. 'Cup of tea,' she muttered to herself. 'That's what you need after being unexpectedly catapulted forward through time thousands of years. A good cup of tea.'

'What she needs,' Angus replied, 'is to be dropped off home in ***Ancient Egypt***, where she belongs!'

'Well, I can't take her home, can I?' Steam began to pour from the spout of the kettle as Marge rummaged in a tin for tea bags. 'Not until I've fixed the time machine, anyway.'

'And how long's that going to take?' Angus looked nervously at Akila, who was staring ahead of her with a blank expression.

'I dunno, a week? Two, maybe?'

'And what are we supposed to do with a real-life Ancient Egyptian in the meantime?'

'Well, that's ***your problem***, isn't it?' Marge placed her hands on her hips. 'You were the one who badgered me to take you to Ancient Egypt. You'll have to tell your parents you've got a friend staying with you.'

'But, but . . .' sputtered Angus. 'I've got to go to school!'

'Well, take her with you!'

'And say what? That's a pretty weird Show and Tell, isn't it? Here's a girl from the lost city of Thonis in the fourth century BC?'

'Well, just say she's an exchange student or something.'

'Two thousand years,' pointed out Angus, 'is quite an exchange!'

CHAPTER 9

UNEXPECTED EGYPTIAN IN BAGGING AREA

Akila gave a sudden shiver. 'I'm still not quite clear about where we are,' she said, 'but wherever it is, it's absolutely freezing! How do you survive it?'

Angus realized with a shock that Akila was still dressed in nothing but a rough white cloth tunic and a pair of sandals. 'I can't take her home like this,' he told Marge. 'It's going to be bad enough trying to convince my parents I've got an exchange student with me. What are they going to say if she turns up in Ancient Egyptian **fancy dress** into the bargain?'

Marge looked Akila up and down. 'Mmmm,' she said, pursing her lips in thought. 'I suppose you're right. Come on then, you two.' Beckoning, she led them towards a security door at one end of the storeroom.

'Where are we going?' asked Angus, leading Akila along with him.

Marge was punching some numbers into a keypad. 'To get her some warmer clothes, of course,' she replied. 'One benefit of working at this **ancient** supermarket,' she went on, 'is that I know all the security codes. Well, I do now that Hattie's hacked into their computer systems.'

'**You're welcome,**' added Hattie's voice through his earpiece. And, with a beep and a *thunk*, the security door opened.

Chances are, you've never been inside a completely empty supermarket. Angus hadn't. And Akila certainly hadn't. Her eyes lit up in wonder as Marge switched on the lights, illuminating aisle after aisle of neatly stacked goods. 'What is this place?' she whispered, looking just as spellbound as an explorer finding their way into an Ancient Egyptian tomb for the first time. Only instead of gold and mummies, she was looking down the biscuit aisle. Which, to be fair, is quite a sight if you've never seen a biscuit before. Try and imagine it next time you're out shopping.

'This way,' said Marge, leading them towards the far end of the store where the clothing aisle was. Akila trotted off in pursuit, looking constantly to either side and clearly desperate to do some more exploring. 'Here we are!' Marge threw out an arm in a '**ta-da**' kind of gesture, pointing down a row of tops and jeans.

'So, I can just take what I need?' asked Akila, wide-eyed.

'Well, for now you can, dear, yes,' said Marge. 'I'll keep the labels and pay for it all in the morning. But generally, no, you can't just help yourself to things from the shops. They have laws about that in this time period. It wasn't until the **sixty-eighth century** that they got past all this buying and selling nonsense. But that's another story.'

Angus wanted to hear this story, but Akila gave another shiver and he felt that, for the moment, it was more important that she was dressed appropriately for the weather and – indeed – the century she was about to spend some time in. Within a few minutes he had helped her pick out a pair of jeans, some white sneakers and a bright pink hoodie. 'Still chilly,' she complained when she came back from the toilets, having changed into the new clothes.

'What about a coat and a scarf, then?' asked Angus, looking at her in surprise. With her head shaved apart from the thick braid and her black Egyptian eye make-up still on, she looked **very cool** and surprisingly modern.

'Don't know what a coat or a scarf is,' said Akila, 'but if they're warm, I want them.' And so, two minutes later, she had completed her outfit with a thick black duffle coat and a long, multicoloured stripy scarf, which she wound around her neck several times.

'You look just like a time traveller, dear,' Marge said, congratulating her. 'Oh, and you'll need this,' she added, handing Akila one of the earpieces that connected to Hattie the computer. 'Now, get out of here, you two. I need to start working on the trolley. As soon as that wheel's fixed we can take Akila home, and you –' she pointed a finger at Angus's chest – 'can **stop bothering me**.'

As they crossed the road to his house, Angus wondered how on earth he was going to explain to his parents that he had a friend staying with him. But, in the end, it was far less complicated than he'd feared.

'Exchange student?' said his mum, brushing back her hair and looking up from the book she was poring over. 'Erm, did you tell me about it?'

'Yeah, I think there was a letter last week, from school?' Angus raised his eyebrows in an expression of pure innocence.

'Was there?' His mum looked confused. 'Well, if there was, it's gone clean out of my head. Sorry.' She smiled brightly at Akila. '**Hello!** Welcome to our country,' she said, loudly and slowly.

Akila, of course, was now wearing the earpiece that allowed Hattie to translate for her. 'Thanks,' she replied briskly. 'Nice to be here. It's very interesting – very different to home, I can tell you that!'

'She, er, she speaks excellent English,' explained Angus needlessly.

'Your house is very, erm . . .' Akila looked around at the lights on the ceiling, the TV, the windows, the books on the table . . . All things, of course, that she had never encountered in her life before. 'Well, it's ***mind-blowing***, really,' she said faintly.

Angus's parents were proud of their little house, but they had never heard it called 'mind-blowing' before. 'I'm glad you think so,' his mum replied, looking a little suspicious, as if Akila might be making fun of her. 'Angus, why don't you make your friend something to eat. She must be hungry after her long journey. How long was your journey, by the way?' she added.

'You literally have no idea,' Akila replied. 'Like, hundreds of years. At least.'

'I think she's a bit ***jet-lagged***,' gabbled Angus, grabbing Akila by the shoulders and steering her towards the kitchen before the conversation became any weirder. 'Come on,' he said to her quietly. 'If you think this stuff is cool, just wait until I make you my famous fish-finger sandwich. That really will blow your mind.'

*

The following morning, after she'd been introduced to the concept of Coco Pops for the first time ever, Akila and Angus set off for school. 'You're taking this pretty calmly, considering,' he told her as they walked.

'Well, Marge and Hattie explained it all to me,' she told him. 'And I absolutely love finding out about other places. My dad's a merchant, remember? Whenever he comes back from a voyage he tells me tales about the people he's met and the things he's seen. Like, once he went all the way to Nubia and brought me back a bow and arrows. They're the best archers in the world, Nubians.'

'I reckon you'll be able to top all your dad's stories when you explain the biscuit aisle in the supermarket to him,' Angus pointed out.

'I think it's fair to say it'll absolutely blow his mind, yes,' she agreed. 'Not that anyone's ever going to ***believe me***, of course. What's with your mum and dad, though?' she asked suddenly. 'They don't seem that interested in you.'

Angus felt himself blushing. 'They're just busy,' he mumbled. 'Mum's going for this big promotion, you know? And Dad's working a lot, so he's tired. I'm fine, though.'

Akila had stopped walking and placed her hands on her hips. 'I don't think you are fine,' she told him, meeting his eye with an unnervingly steady gaze. 'I think you're a bit ***lonely***.'

'Wow,' said Angus, blushing even harder. 'You really tell it like it is in Ancient Egypt, don't you?'

'What's the point in acting any other way?' she asked. 'Life's too short, you know?'

HI, KIDS, FACT PIG here. Akila's right! Do you know what the average life expectancy was for someone in Ancient Egypt?

GO AWAY, FACT PIG! They can look that up for themselves. On with the story.

*Fact Pig gives a wounded ***oink*** and walks off huffily*

'Come on, then,' Angus told Akila, finally breaking eye contact after a long moment and leading her off down the street. 'And remember, you're my exchange student from Egypt. Try not to talk to too many people. If you run out of paper, don't get excited and ask the teacher for another piece of papyrus. And hopefully it won't take Marge too long to repair the trolley and we can get you home.'

'I hope it takes ages,' Akila replied airily, looking around her in fascination. 'This place is so ***splendidly odd***. I want to find out all about it.'

Ms Bancroft was absolutely delighted to find out that she had an actual, real girl from Egypt in her lesson about the Ancient Egyptians. 'And, are you interested in your country's history, dear?' she asked Akila as soon as Angus introduced her. 'Have you been to a museum, and seen any of the statues and artefacts that your ancestors might have worshipped? I mean –' she gave a smile that meant a bad history-teacher joke was incoming – 'the mummy of your mummy's mummy's mummy's mummy's mummy's mummy could well have been . . . a ***mummy!***'

'Erm . . . no,' Akila replied. She had, of course, seen hundreds of statues, but never in a museum. 'And I don't think my mummy would ever have been mummified,' she added. 'That's just for the poshos. It costs an absolute fortune, you know. I've always thought it's a waste of good bandages, to be honest.'

'Right,' replied Ms Bancroft with a slightly nervous laugh. 'Let's get on with the lesson, shall we? I'm sure Akila will have lots more insights to share with us as we discover what daily life was like for ordinary people in Ancient Egypt.'

Akila did, indeed, have lots of insights to share with Ms Bancroft as she began to teach her carefully researched lesson. Those insights can be summed up in the simple phrase, 'You're talking a load of absolute rubbish.'

'**No**, **no**, **no**,' Akila said after a couple of minutes. 'That's not the hieroglyph for "river".'

'Well, I'm fairly sure it is, actually,' replied the teacher, looking flustered. 'This tablet was discovered on the banks of the Nile, and it says that this is the shrine of a river god.'

'No, it doesn't,' countered Akila. 'That says "this drinking trough is for ***donkeys only***"!' The class erupted into loud laughter.

'This isn't exactly *keeping a low profile*, is it?' hissed Angus as Ms Bancroft, scarlet-faced, turned back towards her whiteboard. 'Try and keep your thoughts to yourself, OK? People are going to start asking questions about why my foreign exchange student is suddenly fluent in ancient hieroglyphs!' Akila gave a reluctant nod and sat fairly quietly for the remainder of the class. She did let out the occasional **snort** of disagreement – especially when Ms Bancroft talked about people riding around Ancient Egypt on camels. 'Nobody *rides* camels where I come from,' she hissed at Angus. 'They ride donkeys!' But he silenced her with a glare.

Akila, as you might expect, found school completely fascinating. Especially the science lesson that afternoon, when the teacher showed them how to make hydrogen using a chemical reaction. She used it to fill a balloon, which floated upward until the teacher set light to it with a taper and it exploded with a flash of flame and a loud bang.

'**Whoa!**' Akila exclaimed, earning a titter from some of the other girls nearby.

'Sounds like she's never seen a balloon before,' added one with a snort. But Akila didn't care. She was intent on finding out as much as she could. And her reaction to the balloon was nothing compared to her squeal of delight on Thursday when the science teacher wheeled the Van der Graaf Generator out of the cupboard. 'Look at me!' cried Akila, pressing her finger to the glass ball so her long dark hair stood up on end. 'I'm Hathor!'

QUICK NOTE FROM **FACT PIG**

Hathor is an Ancient Egyptian goddess who is often wearing a big headdress like **cow's horns** in her pictures and statues. Now please read on. I'm busy. Someone's just filled my trough with leftover goulash.

*

Every evening after school, Angus took Akila to the supermarket to check on Marge as she worked on the Time Trolley. Usually she was lying underneath it with a welding torch and shooed them away. 'It'll be ready when it's ready,' she told them. 'One thing you need to learn about time travel – there's no use being **impatient**. Everything happens in its own time!' And so, while they waited, Angus spent the time at home chatting to Akila. His parents had been so busy and tired recently it actually surprised him how nice it was to have someone to hang out with in the evenings. Akila was curious about everything, friendly and funny, and to his surprise she even got on famously with McQueen. 'I thought you'd only like **cats**,' he said. 'That's what my history textbook said, anyway.'

Akila gave a sniff. 'I think we've discovered that your textbooks leave a lot to be desired,' she told him. 'Sure, lots of people have cats, but we have pet dogs too. Very useful for hunting.'

As the week went on, Angus found himself learning more and more about where Akila came from. She told him more about her father's journeys and the gifts and stories he brought back with him. Despite the fact that this was, technically, a history lesson, Angus found it fascinating. And, as you'd expect, his actual history homework was becoming ***seriously impressive***. In return, he told Akila lots about the present day and spent hours playing board games with her – something which, he'd discovered to his surprise, was very popular in Ancient Egypt.

She tried to teach him a game called Senet, using his chess set for the playing pieces, but he never did manage to get his head around the complicated rules. 'To be fair,' she told him, 'the rules do vary depending on where you come from.' Akila, on the other hand, mastered chess surprisingly quickly, and by the end of the week she was beating him regularly. He also tried to show her a few games on his phone, but she found it surprisingly uninteresting. 'What's the point of playing a game when you can't ***touch*** the pieces?' she asked him, before laying out the chessboard once again.

Every day, without fail, Angus pestered Marge for an update on her repairs to the Time Trolley. 'It'll be ready when it's ready,' she told him again, brandishing a hammer. 'This technology from your time period is really hard to work with, you know! I can't just magic a Time Guidance Directional Matrix out of thin air!'

'I bet my uncle could have done it,' Akila broke in. 'He's very handy. Built his own ox cart from scratch.'

'This is a bit more complicated than an ox cart,' Marge told her sternly. Akila and Angus exchanged a grin.

'Careful, Marge,' Angus told her cheekily. 'You're talking to someone from the civilization that built the ***pyramids***. She might be able to tell you a thing or two about engineering.' Marge chased them crossly from the workshop.

Angus and Akila had become such firm friends by the end of the second week that he actually felt a huge pang of disappointment when Marge triumphantly declared that the Time Trolley was ready.

'I'm pretty sure I've sorted out that wheel,' she told them one evening, bursting through the storeroom door wiping oil from her hands with a rag. 'And Hattie says she's almost certain that we can get Akila home safely. After that –' she pointed at Angus sternly – 'you're ***on your own***, OK? No more jaunts into history to help with your homework.'

Akila's face fell. 'You'll come and visit, though,' she said quietly. 'Right?'

'Yeah, Marge,' said Angus. 'We can swing by when you're out stocking up your cheese counter, can't we?'

Excitement filled him at the prospect of Akila showing him round Ancient Egypt until he noticed Marge looking at them both with a sad expression.

'Listen,' she told him. 'Like I said, I wasn't really supposed to be using the time machine anyway. So I've decided that, after this one last trip to put things right, I'd better follow my own advice and stop popping back and forth. My customers are going to be ***very disappointed***, though. There's a goat's cheese they stopped making in the early eighteenth century, and Mrs Nelmes is quite addicted to it. Ah, well.' She gave a large sigh and dusted her hands together. 'It is what it is, I suppose. Right, you two. Say your farewells and meet me in the car park at ten o'clock. It's home time for Little Miss Ancient Egypt here.'

Akila came back to Angus's house for a final twenty-first-century tea. During her fortnight there she'd developed a taste for some, though not all, of the foods Angus liked. But her absolute favourite was ***fish fingers***. She simply couldn't get enough of them. 'I mean, back in Ancient Egypt, fish haven't even evolved fingers yet!' she had enthused when she'd tried them for the first time. 'And who knew they'd be so delicious? How many fingers does each fish have, anyway? Or does it vary by species?' More than a little reluctantly, Angus had to explain that the name didn't actually mean that fish had developed digits. (Although for the rest of his life he was unable to eat a fish finger without thinking how cool it would be if they did. And now, neither will you. You're welcome.)

Angus and Akila carried their tea through to the living room, where his mum was tapping away furiously at her laptop, the table in front of her piled high with notebooks. His dad was slumped on the sofa as usual and looked half asleep in the dim, flickering light from the TV screen. The local news was on and a very earnest-looking young reporter was standing in the town's main square.

'Behind me, you can see the town hall,' he was saying, 'and, next to the clock tower, something that the mayor has called a ***total outrage***.' The camera zoomed in past his shoulder, wavering as it tracked upwards to the clock tower on the roof of the hall. And there, balanced right near the huge white clock face, was a shopping trolley. Angus and Akila exchanged a surprised look.

'However did ***that*** get up there?' gasped Angus's mum, looking up absent-mindedly from her work.

'Students, probably,' his dad replied. 'Any more ketchup over there, Angus?' By this time, the news report had moved on to something else – and in his anxiety about the journey to come, Angus forgot all about the mystery of the trolley on the town-hall roof. (Which is a shame because, as you will no doubt have worked out for yourself, it's ***incredibly important*** to the plot and will feature heavily in a few chapters' time when it plays a pivotal role in this story. We don't just chuck these things in for no reason, you know.)

That night, Angus reluctantly led Akila out of the storeroom and into the dark car park, where Marge was already sitting in the trolley, talking to Hattie. 'Systems online?' she asked.

'**I won't really know until we start moving,**' the computer replied. '**That's the thing about time travel, you see. You don't really know whether it's working or not until you start actually travelling through time. Up until then it's quite a lot of guesswork.**'

'This isn't exactly filling me with confidence, Hattie,' said Angus as he and Akila climbed into the front of the trolley and sat down, hands wrapped around their knees in preparation for take-off.

'**Oh, don't worry,**' the computer replied. '**I'm almost certain this has a relatively high chance of working. Possibly.**'

'Relatively?' squeaked Akila, excited at the prospect of ending up somewhere else completely different.

'**Well, this is time travel,**' Hattie told her. '**Everything's relative.**'

'Possibly?' added Angus.

'**And anything's possible,**' Hattie went on. '**Starting the launch cycle. Stand by.**'

With a clanking and a rattling, the shopping trolley began to ***lurch forward*** down the steep slope of the car park. The orange lights overhead began to flash past faster and faster. Angus peered out through half-closed eyes. 'Is it holding?' he asked.

'**So far, so good,**' Hattie replied. '**We're up to 6.8 miles an hour. Prepare for time jump. Here . . . we . . . go . . .**'

At that moment, there was a fizz of static and the trolley gave an alarming lurch. 'What's going on?' shrieked Marge desperately.

'**Some kind of signal's locked on to us,**' replied Hattie. '**It's overriding my guidance systems! Our destination is being changed.**'

'No, no, no!' moaned Marge. 'This is exactly the reason I wasn't supposed to be using the time machine.

Abort take-off! ABORT! ABORT!'

'**Too late,**' Hattie told her. '**Hold on!**'

'What's going on?' shouted Angus, as sparks and flashes began to run up and down the metal sides of the trolley.

'He found me!' wailed Marge. 'I don't know how, but he found me!'

'Who found you?' asked Akila. 'What's going on?'

'***New destination locked*. Prepare for time jump.**' Hattie broke in. And before Marge could explain, the trolley disappeared from the car park, leaving a double trail of multi-coloured flames across the tarmac.

CHAPTER 10

WELCOME TO THE NINETY-NINTH CENTURY

Generally in life, it's less than ideal when a computer starts repeating the word 'Warning'. This being the case, none of the occupants of the Time Trolley were very encouraged by what happened shortly after they disappeared from the supermarket car park and entered the time void.

'**Warning.**' said Hattie the computer. '**Warning. Warning.**'

'That can't be good,' said Marge, looking worried.

'***Warning***,' added Hattie, just for good measure.

'Yes, thank you, Hattie,' Marge told her. 'We heard you the first three times. Warning. We get it.'

'***Warning***,' repeated the computer.

'***I KNOW!***' Marge's temper snapped. 'You've said "warning" several times. What are you warning us about?'

'**Guidance systems have been overridden**,' explained Hattie, who didn't seem as chatty as usual. '**New destination confirmed**,' added un-chatty Hattie. '**Re-routing to the ninety-ninth century**.'

'***WHAT?***' At this, Marge clutched at her curly hair in alarm. 'No, no, no! ***No! NO!***'

'What's going on?' Angus wanted to know. 'What does she mean, guidance systems have been overridden?'

'Oh, come on,' said Akila. 'I'm from thousands of years in the past and even I understood that. She means that something's taken over Hattie and is sending us to a different destination. Right?'

'Right,' said Marge. And Angus realized that, for the first time, she looked really frightened. 'Hattie's taking us back to the far future – the place where the time machine was first invented. My home.'

'What – the ninety-ninth century?' Angus's head buzzed with excitement. 'We're going to see how things turn out for the human race? Will everybody be whizzing around on jet packs?'

'Why does everyone from your time obsess about the future being full of jet packs?' Marge wanted to know. 'Is that really all you're bothered about?'

'Just thought it would be cool,' said Angus, stung.

'I mean, they did have jet packs back in the twenty-third century,' added Marge. 'But they were very impractical and ***incredibly dangerous***. You know those electric scooters that were all the rage in your time? Well, imagine those but at hundreds of metres in the air and with no traffic lights. It didn't end well.'

'I'm still excited about seeing the future,' said Angus, clinging to the front of the trolley as it whizzed through the blackness.

'Technically, I've seen the future already,' Akila reminded him. 'And it was very cold. I hope it's not even colder here.' She wrapped her stripy scarf more tightly around her neck.

'You don't understand!' Marge's eyes were wide with fear. 'The Time Trolley can't go back to the future! It can't! I'm supposed to be ***hiding it*** . . . from *him*! That's the reason I took it all the way back to the A.I. period in the first place – I thought he'd never look for me there!'

'Why do you call our time the A.I. period?' Angus had been meaning to ask this ever since he'd heard Marge and Hattie using the expression. 'Is it because we invented Artificial Intelligence, or . . .'

But he never got the chance to finish his question. Marge had started talking to the time machine's computer in an urgent tone. 'Hattie, override all systems. Do you understand me? Do not, I repeat, do not return this technology to the ninety-ninth century. Override! ***Now!***'

'**Override not possible,**' Hattie replied. '**And, yes, I'm fully aware that wasn't the response you were looking for. But it's out of my hands. Not that I have hands, as I'm a sophisticated computer program. But if I did have hands, it would be out of them.**'

'This is ***NOT HELPING***,' Marge informed her crossly.

'**I could say "warning" a few more times?**' Hattie suggested.

'Who are you hiding the Time Trolley from?' Angus wanted to know.

'You really, really don't want to know,' Marge told him. 'Let's just get there, turn around and ***get straight out again***. No exploring the future, get it?'

'Fine,' Angus agreed grumpily. He'd been really excited about having a proper look around the far future, rather than just sitting in it quietly while Marge repaired the wheel. But, he supposed, she was the time-travel expert. And whoever she was scared of in the ninety-ninth century, they clearly weren't someone he was particularly keen on bumping into. (**SPOILER ALERT:** he's about to do

exactly that but don't tell anyone. It'll ruin the dramatic end to this chapter.)

With a flash, the Time Trolley rematerialized. But this time, rather than overturning into a bush or on a sand dune, it was suddenly flying smoothly through a clear blue summer sky. '**Time coordinates – ninety-ninth century,**' said Hattie calmly. '**Temporal jump achieved. We're being guided in. And isn't it nice to be home?**' With a jolt, Angus realized that he was now thousands of years in the future. Scrambling up on to his knees, he peered over the edge of the trolley, desperate to take everything in during the short time they'd apparently be here.

A gleaming, spotless city spread out beneath them. Angus had been expecting something futuristic – lots of glass-and-chrome skyscrapers, probably with people whizzing around wearing jet packs. But, instead, the buildings looked like they were made of brick. Several large areas of parkland could be seen breaking up the city streets, and a glistening ribbon of blue wound its way right through the centre – a wide, slow-flowing river. Angus took a deep breath in and actually gasped with shock. The air was incredibly fresh and clean – it made him feel like he'd been breathing right next to a truck's exhaust pipe for most of his life up until now. A **blush** crept up his cheeks as he thought about how the rest of history would view his own generation, if only they knew. Then, with a glance at Marge, he realized that some of them *did* know, and he decided he might be better off not learning what those letters A.I. stood for, after all.

Hattie's voice interrupted his gloomy thoughts. '**Preparing to dock at the Imperium,**' said the computer. '**Stand by.**'

'What's the ***Imperium?***' asked Akila.

'The palace of the Planetary Emperor,' Marge replied quietly, still looking terrified. 'It's where I used to work. Look.' She pointed ahead of them. There, on the outskirts of the city, stood a gigantic pyramid constructed of huge blocks of stone. Large windows and balconies were set into the sloping walls, with green plants spilling over their edges.

'**Ooooh**,' said Angus and Akila at exactly the same time. (Saying 'ooh' at moments such as these is a human reaction that transcends all boundaries of time.)

'Well, I say "palace of the Planetary Emperor",' Marge went on, sounding tense. 'But what I actually mean is: the palace of the ***extremely evil Planetary Emperor***. The evil Emperor Kragg, to be precise.'

'Evil emperor?' asked Angus. That didn't sound good. In reply, Marge pointed downwards, and he got unsteadily to his feet to see what she was indicating. The huge pyramid was surrounded on all sides by a **gigantic army**.

He couldn't make out all the details, but there seemed to be trucks with missiles on them, guard towers with searchlights and what looked suspiciously like battalions of robots lined up in formation. 'What's going on down there?' he breathed.

'I told you,' replied Marge. 'This is the HQ of the evil Emperor Kragg. He's about to launch an invasion, which will spark something called the Great Whole Earth War. He's spent years gathering all kinds of military technology to launch his attack, together with his chief scientist, Doctor Proteus.'

'He sounds weird and creepy,' said Akila with a shiver.

'He is,' Marge told her. 'As well as being very clever and very, very dangerous.'

'There's always a ***weird sidekick***, isn't there?' Angus sighed. Marge nodded in reply. 'And, by the way,' Angus added, 'why do evil people always call themselves such evil names. I mean, Doctor Proteus! It couldn't be any more evil-sidekicky if it tried! If I was a supervillain, I'd at least try and hide the fact. I'd call myself, I don't know . . . Captain Rainbows or something.'

'**Stand by, Captain Rainbows,**' Hattie broke in. '**We're**

coming in to land.' The trolley continued its smooth downward flightpath towards a wide opening at the top of the pyramid. As they approached, Angus could see that they were about to touch down in the centre of a ***gleaming laboratory***, with workbenches and computers arranged around the outside of the room. Thick double doors could be seen beyond this, and he was relieved that they were firmly closed.

'Right, I'm not from around here, so let me check I've got this straight,' said Akila, leaping out of the trolley and looking around her. 'You used to work for this evil emperor? Here in this pyramid? Using all these magical artefacts?'

'Well, I used to, yes,' admitted Marge. 'But you've got to realize, he wasn't always evil. Or at least he pretended not to be. Back when he was just Kragg, he fooled me into bringing my time-travel research here – and he funded my laboratory so I could carry on with the work.' As she spoke, the trolley landed smoothly in the middle of the lab. 'By the time I actually managed to achieve time travel,' she went on, climbing out and looking around suspiciously, 'I'd realized what he ***truly*** was. I didn't have enough evidence to go to the police, but I was sure that I needed to stop him getting his hands on the time machine. So I decided to take it away and hide it somewhere far in the past. Somewhere he'd never think of looking.'

'**And may I say, you're doing a truly amazing job,**' said Hattie.

'Sarcastic computer comments are not what I need right now,' snapped Marge.

'But, how did he ***find*** you?' Angus wanted to know.

'Somehow, he managed to lock on to us from here,' Marge told him. 'Proteus must have used some of my research to search the timeline, find Hattie and take over to force her to bring us here. But not for long.' She began to open drawers in one of the workbenches. 'If I can regain control of Hattie, we can leap right back to the A.I. period before he gets here.'

'This place is incredible!' said Angus, moving to the balcony and looking out across the city. He felt, with only a few minutes to enjoy the far future, that he might as well look around a bit. 'It's so clean!'

'Reminds me of home, actually,' said Akila. 'It's nice they have pyramids here, at least. Why don't people in your time have them? They're really cool, you know.'

Angus thought about this and realized that Akila was right. Pyramids **were** cool. Why didn't people build more pyramids? He shrugged.

'No pyramids in the A.I. period,' Marge told them from the other side of the room. 'They constructed some of the worst buildings ever devised, in fact. Nothing worth saving.' She tutted and dragged a large metal box towards the trolley. Unclipping the top, she pulled out a shining metal device and plugged it into one end of the handle at the back.

'Again, about this A.I. thing . . .' began Angus, but Marge silenced him with an upraised finger. Grabbing a small keyboard from the metal box, she began typing rapidly. 'If I can just disable his signal,' she said tersely, 'we can get out of here.'

'So – why were you hiding the trolley from this Kragg person again?' asked Angus, looking nervously at the metal doors.

'Isn't it obvious?' Marge told him. 'I told you – he's planning to terrorize the entire planet and take it over as dictator! Imagine what he'd be able to do with a time machine! I knew as soon as I invented it that I had to hide it safely away, somewhere he'd never think of looking. Trouble is, now we're right back here with exactly what he wants! This is a free ticket to wherever he wants to go! With a time machine he'll be ***unstoppable!*** He could just keep going backwards and forward until he has whatever he needs!' She shook her head. 'We've got to get away, as quickly as possible.'

'How long is it going to take?' asked Akila, also glancing towards the doors with a scared expression. She had no idea what an evil emperor from the future might look like, but she wasn't especially keen on finding out.

'No more questions,' snapped Marge. 'Just as long as those doors don't slide open, revealing the evil Emperor Kragg, we'll be OK. Don't panic.'

At that point, the doors slid open to reveal the evil Emperor Kragg. '***Now*** can we panic?' asked Angus.

Like Akila, you're probably wondering at this point what an evil emperor from the ninety-ninth century might look like. So here, to gratify your curiosity, is the answer to that question.

Evil Emperor Kragg was two and a half metres tall (that's eight feet, for our grown-up readers). If you're wondering about this, in the far future you can go to a special clinic and easily change your height any time you want. Marge had chosen to be very small by future standards. Kragg, like a typical evil dictator in the making, had decided to go for the maximum height possible. (It says quite a lot about someone, the height they choose to be. But until that technology is invented it's not something you need to worry about. In fact, it's become a distraction from the story. Let's get back to evil Emperor Kragg, shall we?)

Kragg was dressed in a pair of ***gigantic***, shiny black high boots and a pair of black military-style trousers. His torso, which was bare, had a complicated-looking electronic control panel set into one side of the chest, with blinking red and white lights. His right arm was entirely robotic. His left arm, which was thick with muscle, was outstretched, with his hand clenched into a fist, directed at Marge. One eye was made of machinery and it gleamed red. The other eye was narrowed in an expression of triumph below the shining, bald dome of his head.

'So!'

said the evil Emperor Kragg in exactly the sort of voice you'd expect an evil emperor from the year 9824 to have (very deep and throaty, if you need a hint).

'You thought you could hide from me, **traitor!** But nobody can hide from the might of Kragg! I have found you, cowering back there in the A.I. period. And now, I have reclaimed the time device! **I am victorious!**'

'No, you're not,' Marge contradicted him. 'Just ignore me, I'm not really here. Took a wrong turning. **Ha-ha**. We'll be off in a minute. Nothing to see. As you were. Carry on. Shut the door on your way out. Bye-bye, now.'

'Oh, I don't think so,' snarled Kragg, with an evil sneer. 'Nice to see you again, Marganulus 5.'

'Oh, is that what Marge is short for?' said Angus without thinking. 'I assumed it'd be Marjorie. Or possibly Margaret.'

'And who is this annoyance?' Kragg turned on Angus, his robot arm making a hissing noise like bus doors as its machinery activated. 'Should I **eliminate** him?'

'I'd very much rather you didn't,' said Marge calmly.

'Seconded,' added Akila.

'Thirded,' Angus chipped in meekly.

'Because I could, you know,' Kragg continued, raising the gleaming metal arm. 'I could wipe him out, just like *that.*' As he spoke, a bright blue bolt of electricity fired from the end of the arm, blasting a large, smoking hole in the outside wall of the pyramid.

'Ooh, ***laser arms***,' said Angus. 'Cool.'

'Did it work?' came a new voice from the corridor outside. The voice was thin and reedy, with a wheedling tone. 'I heard shooting. I bet you hit it, whatever it was. You're such a good shot.'

'Oh, shut up, Proteus,' roared Kragg. 'Shut up and get in here! Enough of your fawning! Yes, it did work. For once, you have not failed me! I have the time device!'

'Excellent,' said the wheedling voice, with a hint of greedy satisfaction. And now a second man appeared in the doorway. But whereas Emperor Kragg was enormous and impressive, this person was small and weedy, with thin greasy hair sticking upwards from his squat head. He had the air of a badly treated dog that still wants to please its master – even though he's the worst master in the world, ever. He was clutching a small device with a screen in one hand, and his dull eyes lit up as he caught sight of the Time Trolley and Marge kneeling beside it. 'Aha!' he squealed. 'It *did* work. I latched on to the correct coordinates, overrode the computer and brought the time device here to you! ***I am a genius!***'

'Yes, yes –' Kragg, who like all supervillains didn't like his sidekick getting too much attention, waved his robot arm in frustration – 'we've done all that before you came in.' Out of the corner of his eye, Angus caught Marge beckoning to him and Akila. She nodded at them, with an expression that said: *I've hacked back into the trolley so we can escape. Get in now and let's get out of here.* It's hard to say all that with one expression but she's from the future and they're very good at expressions.

'I do apologize, Your Evility,' said Proteus. 'I didn't mean to offend.'

'***SILENCE***, you blithering fool!'

While the two villains bickered, Angus sauntered in as casual a manner as he could manage towards the shopping trolley, grabbing Akila by the hand as he went. As they joined Marge in the centre of the laboratory, she got to her feet.

'**STOP THEM!**' screeched Kragg, seeing what was happening.

'Into the trolley!' countered Marge. '***Go, go, go!*** Before they can stop us!' Angus and Akila leapt in, with Marge scrambling in behind them. 'Emergency protocol, Hattie!' she shouted. 'Get us out of here!'

'**Immediate temporal resolve,**' confirmed Hattie. '**Stand by for time jump in *five seconds*.**' Angus judged the distance between the trolley and the two men in the doorway. *Surely*, he thought, *there is no way they can cover that distance in a mere five seconds*. It had to be fifty metres away. Nevertheless, Kragg and Proteus had both begun to sprint towards them.

'**Two ... one ...**' continued Hattie. '**Zero!**' And, with the usual flash of energy, the trolley vanished.

What neither Angus, Akila nor Marge had noticed, however, was that something rather alarming had happened between Hattie saying 'one' and the crucial 'zero'. And the rather alarming thing that had happened was this:

Evil Emperor Kragg's robot arm, you see, wasn't just a laser cannon. It had several different functions, not unlike one of those very elaborate penknives that people take camping with them. It was a corkscrew, a toothpick, a wireless speaker (even evil emperors need to relax with a few tunes every now and then) and also – and this is the relevant part here – a hugely powerful telescopic grabbing tool. Before the trolley had a chance to vanish back into the time void, the end of the robot arm shot out in a flash and fastened itself firmly to the handle of the trolley. With his other arm, Kragg grabbed his oily sidekick and, together, they were dragged along after the trolley as it disappeared with a *whoosh* into the past.

'**Guidance systems restored,**' said Hattie as the trolley careered backwards through the void. '**Returning to the *Age of the Idiot*.**'

'Sorry,' said Angus above the roaring of the wind. 'Excuse me please, sorry, didn't quite catch that. The age of the *what*?'

CHAPTER 11

THE AGE OF THE IDIOT

BANG! SWOOSH! FZZZRT! SQUITCH! PHLAM! Those are the noises that time travel makes. Nothing we can do about it, it just does. The Time Trolley materialized in the grey, drizzly sky above Angus's hometown and, despite the immediate mouthful of dirty, petrol-scented air, he felt a surge of relief. Not quite big enough, though, to extinguish the sense of outrage at his discovery of what A.I. actually stood for.

'The Age of the ***Idiot?***' he asked Marge, his voice rising to an indignant squawk.

'The Age of the Idiot,' she confirmed with a rather sad-looking nod.

'**Destination achieved,**' added Hattie the computer. '**We are now in the Age of the Idiot.**'

'***The Age of the Idiot?!***' Angus asked her in an even more indignant squawky squawk.

'**The Age of the Idiot,**' Hattie told him.

'Will you all please stop saying "the Age of the Idiot" at each other,' pleaded Akila, 'and do something about the two men hanging off the back of the trolley?'

'Why is it called that?' demanded Angus, feeling oddly protective about his period of history and growing so angry that he didn't pay enough attention straight away to what Akila had just said.

'Well . . .' Marge looked slightly embarrassed, as if she was having to explain to someone that they had a giant bogey the size of an anaconda hanging out right past their knees – which is always awkward. 'I don't quite know how to tell you this, but . . . your part of history isn't really seen as the most impressive, I'm sorry to say. There's a general feeling that you all spent a lot of time arguing with each other online while the environment got trashed. Took hundreds and hundreds of years to get it properly sorted out. All that plastic.

And we never did manage to re-clone the polar bears properly. What a lot of idiots. Present company excluded, dear. I'm sure you're doing your best.' She gave him a kind, if rather forced, smile.

Angus felt himself blushing furiously as the enormity of what the rest of history made of his era came crashing down on him like a partially melted ice cap. 'But, but . . .' he blustered, trying desperately to think of some valuable contribution that his generation might have made to the countless millennia of Planet Earth. 'You know . . . we invented a lot of cool stuff. Phones and things?'

'Yes, I suppose the **toys** you made were quite impressive, in their way,' said Marge doubtfully. 'Not quite as impressive as the people of the thirty-seventh century, who had to replace the Moon. But, yes, quite fun. Well done, you. Sorry, Akila, what was that you said about something hanging off the back of the trolley? **BWAAAARGH!**'

In between the words 'trolley' and 'bwaaaargh' Marge had turned around to see the evil Emperor Kragg clinging firmly to the wire mesh of the shopping trolley with his cybernetic arm and laughing in the most evil fashion you can possibly imagine. Real 'bwa-ha-haaaa' kind of stuff. Give it a go yourself; it's oddly satisfying. See?

'**BWAAAARGH!**' said Marge again. 'Kragg! He's followed us to the Age of the Idiot!'

'Can we stop calling it that?' pleaded Angus.

'Focus!' Marge told him. 'Come back here and help me get rid of him! He mustn't get his hands on the time machine! **Quick!**' Leaning precariously out of the back of the trolley, she tried to prise open Kragg's metal pincer, which was fastened securely round the handle. Angus lunged to grip her round the middle so she didn't topple out. 'It won't budge!' she said tersely.

'Hattie,' said Akila suddenly, 'you know the ***magic*** that you get from the holes in the wall?'

'Are you talking about electricity?' the computer asked her.

'That's it, yes!' Akila smiled brightly. 'Well, you know you keep some of that magic in a box ready for when you need it?'

'You mean, I store electricity in a battery?'

'Exactly! Well, could you put some of that magic on the pole at the back of the chariot where those men are hanging?'

'Let me get this straight,' said Hattie. **'Are you asking if I can re-route some electrical power from my onboard battery pack to the handle of the chariot? Sorry, the trolley?'**

'Errr, yes.'

'Well, why didn't you just say that? Of course I can. I'm a hugely powerful computer. I could do that without any trouble at all.'

'***Bwa-ha-haaa***,' added the voice of the evil Emperor Kragg from behind them. 'I have you now,' he added. 'Thought you could hide in the Age of the Idiot, did you? Well, I'm here now. And there will be no escape. ***Bwa-ha-haaa***.'

'I really don't see what's so funny,' said Marge from between clenched teeth, hammering ineffectually at the metal pincers.

'Well,' Akila was now saying to the computer, '*will* you re-route some el-ec-tri-cal power to the handle?'

'**It's hard to say,**' Hattie replied. '**It's possible, I suppose. But I don't predict the future, you know. I just travel there. It depends whether somebody asks me to, really.**'

'***Graaargh!***' howled Angus in frustration. 'Hattie! Re-route electrical power to the handle! NOW!'

'**"Please" would be nice.**'

'PLEASE!'

'**Oh, all right, then.**'

Just as Angus hooked Marge upward out of the way, a bolt of bright electricity fizzed across the handle of the trolley. Kragg's claw was forced open and the emperor, still clutching the weedy form of Doctor Proteus to his left-hand side like a disturbing doll, vanished downwards towards a park that was visible below them. 'You can't hide for long!' he roared as he fell. 'I will find you, Marganulus Five! And then . . . I will have my ***revengggge!*** Bblbbrrrrbbble.' (This final noise was because he had fallen into a lake.)

The trolley flew on, soon passing over the grey roof of Hyper-Buy before coming neatly in to land in the car park. 'I think, all things considered,' said Marge, climbing out, 'that our mission to take Akila home to Ancient Egypt was not an unqualified success.'

'Not really, no,' the Egyptian girl agreed, hopping out to join her. 'Instead, we seem to have accidentally brought a super-powerful villain back to this time from the far future.'

'Not ideal, really, is it?' said Angus, feeling a little worried that a simple piece of history homework now seemed to have ballooned into a problem that could threaten the entire history of the human race. 'What are we going to do?'

'I need to think about that,' said Marge grimly. 'Firstly, let's get the trolley inside. We can't let Kragg find it. And we need to keep a ***low profile*** while I figure out what to do. He'll be trying to track us down and we need to make that as difficult as possible.'

Meanwhile, in a park not far away, evil Emperor Kragg emerged from the lake, annoying several swans. Clutching Doctor Proteus, he waded to the bank and sat down on a bench, grinning an evil grin. 'At last, Proteus,' he gloated. 'At last, we have located the time device – right here in the Age of the Idiot, where it's been hiding all the while. And soon I shall take control of the device and rule all of time. Things could not be more perfect.'

'Apart from the fact that you've got a fish flapping in your trousers,' said Doctor Proteus, taking off his white coat and wringing it out on the footpath. Kragg looked down to see that a sizeable koi carp had, indeed, become trapped in one of the pockets of his black army trousers. He grasped it firmly and lifted it to his face. 'Where can I find Marganulus Five?' he asked the fish aggressively. '***Take me to her!***'

'The fish cannot answer you, sir,' Proteus told him apologetically.

'Can't it?' Kragg threw the carp away angrily – fortunately in the direction of the lake. 'I thought it would have evolved the power of speech by now.'

'We're in the past, my lord, not the future,' his sidekick pointed out.

'Ah, yes.' Kragg pondered this for a moment. 'In that case, bring me a jet pack and a ***mark-VII photon plasma matrix generator!***'

'None of those things have been invented, Your Mightiness,' replied Doctor Proteus. 'And besides, jet packs are extremely dangerous.'

'What?' Kragg got to his feet angrily. 'No jet packs yet? What kind of primitive civilization is this? Have they invented anything useful?'

'It isn't called the Age of the Idiot for nothing,' Proteus pointed out.

'In that case,' said Kragg, shaking some water from his robotic arm and lifting it up dramatically, 'we'll have to do this the old-fashioned way. No, not the old-fashioned way. That's not the expression I want. The way that is old-fashioned in the far future. The ***new-fashioned*** way. The way that has not yet been fashioned, but once it has been, it will become old . . . in several thousand years' time. At least . . .' He stopped in frustration. Time travel can play havoc with figures of speech.

'Are you talking about shooting people with your laser cannon until they tell you where Marganulus Five is hiding?' asked Proteus meekly. (It's wise not to upset an evil emperor when he's got his laser-blasting right arm pointed anywhere near you.)

'***Yes! That!*** Let's do that!' Kragg's eyes gleamed wickedly. 'And anybody who stands in our way will meet the same fate as that duck.'

'Which duck?'

'That one over there.' Kragg gestured towards the pond.

'What, the one with the green head?'

'No, not that one. The one with a little tufty bit. To the left of the one with the green head.'

'Ah, yes. That duck.'

'You've put me off, now. What was I saying?'

'You said that anyone who stands in our way will meet the same fate as that duck. Then I said, "Which duck?"'

'Yes, yes, yes!' Kragg motioned impatiently. 'Yes . . . they will meet the same fate as that little tufty duck. ***Ah-ha-ha-ha-haaaa.***' Holding out his robotic arm towards the lake, he placed his other hand on his hip and braced himself, head thrown back in a gesture of evil triumph. But instead of a flash of light and the smell of roasted duck, what happened next was precisely nothing. '***Blast!***' said Kragg, shaking his arm angrily. 'The energy supply to my laser cannon has become depleted. Proteus, bring the charger!'

Doctor Proteus shifted his feet uncomfortably. 'I'm very sorry to say, Your Awfulness,' he said awkwardly, 'that in our haste to follow Marganulus Five through the time vortex, I fear I may have been neglectful in the manner of placing the aforementioned charging device in an appropriate holdall or other carriage vessel.'

'**What?!**' raged the evil Emperor Kragg. 'Are you saying you didn't bring it? Why not?'

'Well –' Proteus made a weedy attempt to stick up for himself – 'you grabbed me in a not inconsiderably un-abrupt fashion and we were summarily, not to put too fine a point on it, pulled through the fabric of time itself behind the Marganulus Device. It's not like I had a chance to pack an overnight bag.' He gave a small laugh, which disappeared into the angry silence like a tiny pebble being tossed into the exact geographical centre of the Pacific Ocean.

'This is ***disastrous!***' raged Kragg. 'This is the first chance I've had in ages to stomp about the place blasting people with my laser cannon! And the stupid thing's got a flat battery! We need to find some way of charging it . . . ***NOW!*** And also a sandwich.'

'A sandwich, Your Hideousness?'

'Yes, a sandwich,' confirmed the evil villain from the far future. 'I'm ***absolutely starving***.'

At the supermarket, Angus and Akila helped Marge push the Time Trolley into its storeroom. Shoving it right to the back, Marge covered it with a large sheet of material. 'Right, you two,' she told them. 'Go home and keep quiet, OK? I need to think this through. And, more importantly, I need to take a proper look at that wheel. I managed a quick repair in my workshop, but it needs fixing for good. Then we'll have to make a plan to get Kragg back to the ninety-ninth century, where he belongs.'

'It's very ***dramatic***, this, isn't it?' said Akila excitedly. 'It's like something out of a carving!'

Authors' Note: This is the Ancient Egyptian equivalent of somebody from our time saying, 'It's like a film,' or something like that. Here are a few others:

He's one sandwich short of a picnic
= he's one block short of a pyramid.

He's not the sharpest knife in the drawer
= he's not the most intricately carved
mural in the tomb.

Let's go back to the drawing board
= let's make a new sheet of papyrus out of reeds.

It's not rocket science
= it's not deciphering hieroglyphs.

He's as thick as two short planks
= he's as thick as the layer of silt
on the bottom of the River Nile.

'I don't know about that, dear,' said Marge doubtfully. 'If Kragg gets hold of that trolley, it's ***game over***.' This, at least, Akila understood. As we know, she played many games back in Egypt, including Senet. She nodded seriously.

'Come on, Angus,' Akila told her friend. 'Let's leave Marge to it for today. We'll see if we can think of a plan as well,' she told the time-travelling cheese enthusiast as they left the storeroom. 'And we'll come back first thing in the morning to work out our next move!'

'See you then,' said Marge distractedly, looking at the veiled form of the Time Trolley with a very worried expression.

Over at the other side of Hyper-Buy, the large glass doors slid open to reveal two extremely unusual customers. The gaggle of schoolkids around the hot food counter giggled and nudged each other as the gigantic form of Emperor Kragg strode into the store, his black boots squelching dramatically. (They were still full of pond water.) Beside him cringed Doctor Proteus. 'Look at all these **idiots!**' roared Kragg.

'Oi!' replied a customer who was passing by. 'Watch your mouth, big guy. And put a shirt on!'

'**Silence**, idiot!' roared Kragg, brandishing his laser arm before remembering it wasn't working. 'Right.' He turned to Proteus. 'This appears to be some primitive form of vending facility. We can stock up here on nutrients and secure a charging cable for my cybernetic arm. Get a basket.'

Proteus quickly grabbed a plastic wheelie basket from a pile by the door and followed his master as he strode towards a display of sandwiches just inside the shop entrance. 'Egg and cress?' he bellowed. 'What kind of primitive protein-based product is this? Ham and Emmental? What does this even mean?' They don't have Emmental cheese in the far future, so he pronounced it to rhyme with 'elemental'. A lady next to him sniggered. 'Oh, ***never mind***,' raged Kragg, sweeping an armful of sandwiches into the basket and stalking off angrily towards the electronics section. Here, he stared at a display of different charging cables while Proteus jogged across to join him, the basket lurching from side to side as he tried to pull it too fast and one of the wheels got stuck.

'You!' Kragg pointed bossily at a teenage boy who was stacking the shelves nearby. 'Are you employed at this vending facility? ***I require assistance!***'

'What?' said the boy in a reedy voice.

'Do. You. Work. Here?' clarified Kragg.

'Oh,' said the boy. 'Yeah. On Saturdays, yeah. And sometimes in the school holidays. But not next Christmas, right, cos we're going to my nan's? She's had shingles, yeah? And Mum said –'

'SILENCE!' roared Kragg.

'Rude,' muttered the boy, returning to his shelf-stacking.

'Come here!' Kragg commanded him. 'I require assistance! Now!'

'I dunno,' grumbled the supermarket worker, reluctantly getting to his feet. 'One minute he's yelling "silence", then he's asking me to talk. And he didn't even ask about Nan's shingles.'

'SILENCE!' Kragg told him again. 'Now –' he held up the underside of his robot arm, revealing a small socket – 'which of these primitive charging cables do I need to reactivate this? It's similar to the Voltatron 17,000. Only not the 300-pin version. And it needs to supply plasmolulous energy, preferably from a non-flandulent source.'

The boy looked at him blankly.

'Come on, come on,' said Kragg impatiently.

After opening his mouth silently once or twice, the boy opened a drawer beneath the display cabinet. 'We've got, like, Android ones?' he said nervously. 'Or is it, like, Micro-USB? Or this one's got lots of different ends on it? You can use it in the car? Or what about a wireless charger?'

'Do you mean to tell me,' said Kragg threateningly, leaning down to glare into the boy's face, 'that you don't have any kind of Voltatron charger?' He felt a tugging at the back of his belt.

'Ah, sire,' said Proteus quietly, 'I think it's possible that the charger we need may not have been ***invented*** yet. In fact . . . Erm, yes. I think we may be too early for it.'

'Oh, this is ***ridiculous!***' Kragg grabbed a few chargers at random and tossed them angrily into the basket. 'Come with me,' he told his servant. 'Surely you can make one of these work. Let's find a base and develop some evil plans. And eat these sandwiches.'

'Certainly, my lord,' said Proteus, following him towards the checkouts.

(**A note about chargers:** As you may have guessed, several advances in technology will be made between now and the ninety-ninth century. These include, as we know, the development of time travel. But unfortunately, society has still not managed to invent one universal charger that will work on all different devices. It seems a shame, but there you go.)

'Please scan your first item,' said the self-checkout machine as the evil emperor from the distant future approached, followed by his sidekick dragging a wheelie basket full of sandwiches and assorted charging cables.

'What ***primitive idiocy*** is this?' snarled Kragg dramatically, eyeing the machine as if it was a very small and insignificant pimple on the bottom of someone he really, really disliked.

'I believe we need to enter the details of the items we wish to procure into this prehistoric device, Your Foulness,' said Doctor Proteus, handing him a triangular packet bearing the label JUICY CHICKEN TRIO. Kragg waved the sandwiches dismissively across the red glowing panel in front of him and the machine emitted a small beep.

'Ha!' he exclaimed triumphantly. 'This ancient machine is no match for my genius! **Bwa ha h**–'

'Would you like to take advantage of our Meal Deal?' asked the checkout in a bright, enthusiastic voice. 'Just scan a drink and snack to make big savings!'

'Pah! Your antiquated sales techniques are pathetic!' roared Kragg, putting the sandwich in one of the large pockets on the side of his black army trousers.

'Please place the item in the bagging area,' said the checkout politely.

'I will not!' bellowed Kragg. 'I am the evil Emperor Kragg! Terror of the four remaining continents and conqueror of the entire planet! *I* give the orders, **puny robot!**'

'Please place the item in the bagging area,' the checkout repeated.

'Faugh!' With a snort, he retrieved the packet and placed it on the platform to the right of the scanner.

'Unexpected item in the bagging area,' chirruped the

checkout. 'Please replace it in your basket and try again. And don't forget our great Meal Deal!'

'I do NOT,' screeched Kragg, his voice cracking with frustration, 'WANT. A ***MEAL*. *DEAL!***'

'Please place the item in the bagging area.'

'Would you like me to help you, Your Mightiness?' asked Proteus, nervously wringing his hands together.

'I would not,' replied his master in a dangerously quiet voice. 'I am an evil genius from the ninety-ninth century. I have been plotting total planetary domination for years. Moreover, I have just travelled thousands of years through time in order to carry out my terrifying evil plan. I will not be defeated by this irritating, antiquated piece of junk and a warm sandwich!' Leaning forward, he shouted incredibly loudly into the checkout's screen:

'BOW BEFORE ME! FOR I AM KRAGG! AND I WILL NOT BE UPSOLD TO A MEAL DEAL! ALLOW ME TO LEAVE WITH MY COMESTIBLES OR FACE MY WRATH!'

'Please wait,' said the checkout calmly. 'Someone is coming to help you.' A red light on a stalk began to flash.

'Oh, this is ridiculous,' fumed Kragg, tapping a booted foot impatiently. 'I don't have time for this nonsense! I need to locate Marganulus Five . . . what was it that those idiots called her?'

'***Marge***, Your Hideousness,' Proteus chipped in.

'Yes, yes.' Kragg's eyes glittered with cold malice. 'I will locate her before long. And then I shall take my revenge.

Where is she?' he mused, looking around the shop. 'Where is . . . ***Marge?***'

'Marge?' replied the shop assistant who had just come over to help him. 'From the cheese counter? I think she's out the back in the storeroom. Saw her a couple of minutes ago when I went to make a cup of tea, fiddling about with an old shopping trolley.' The man pointed towards the far end of the supermarket. 'Does she know you're coming?' he asked doubtfully, running his eyes over Kragg's gigantic uncovered torso and robot arm.

'Oh no,' said Kragg in a dangerous tone. 'We thought it might be nice to . . . surprise her. ***Bwa-ha-haaaaaaa***.'

'Don't you want this Juicy Chicken Trio?' the assistant shouted after him as he strode away, looking as menacing as it's possible to look while walking down an aisle full of cat food.

CHAPTER 12
STUCK IN THE PAST

The following morning, Angus and Akila burst excitedly into Marge's workshop at the back of the supermarket, with McQueen barking at their heels.

'Morning!' yelled Angus. 'How's the work going? Are you ready to set a trap for Kragg yet? Do you want a cup of tea?' He headed automatically for the trestle table at the back of the room before registering that something was ***very***, ***very wrong***.

Normally, when Marge was working away in the storeroom, the radio would be playing some soft music in the background and the room would be warm and cosy. The kettle would have been generating endless cups of strong tea. This morning, the room was dim and chilly.

The radio was off and the kettle obviously hadn't been used. Something inside Angus's brain registered all these details at once and sent alarm signals clanging away inside his head before his racing feet reached the tea table. 'Akila!' he blurted. '**Look out!** Something's –'

But he never got the chance to finish. A pair of long arms shot out from beneath the tea table. A pair of strong hands (which were attached to the end of said arms) gripped his ankles firmly and pulled. With a startled yelp Angus was planted firmly on his back. The door to the storeroom slammed shut behind Akila, revealing the massive form of Emperor Kragg. 'I have you now, idiots!' he roared gloatingly. As he spoke, Doctor Proteus emerged from beneath the table, cackling with glee.

'Wonderful plan, Your Horribleness!' he said. 'Simply brilliant!'

'What?' said Akila. 'Hiding underneath a table and behind a door? That's an old trick where I come from. And that's thousands of years ago.'

'**Silence!**' bellowed Kragg.

'What have you done with Marge?' demanded Angus furiously. He struggled to rise, but Proteus placed a foot on his chest to stop him.

'Oh, don't worry,' purred the little man sarcastically. 'We've put her in one of her very favourite places. We thought she was so fond of the past we'd give her a little holiday there. A permanent holiday! People always say they don't want their holidays to end. Well, this one never will! Although, come to think of it, if she's staying there forever, it's not technically a holiday. I suppose, strictly speaking, she's emigrated. Well, put it this way –'

'***SHUT UP!***' roared Kragg. 'Or I'll emigrate you!' He had been looking forward to enjoying this moment of evil triumph, and Proteus was in danger of spoiling it by overthinking his 'holiday' speech.

'Where is she?' said Akila angrily, turning on Kragg with her hands on her hips. She had an expression of such anger on her face that the evil dictator actually took a small step backwards, before remembering that he was about to take complete control of the entire planet for all time and didn't need to be afraid of children, even really, really cross ones.

'She's marooned in the past!' Kragg told her with a roar of evil laughter. 'Marooned, I tell you! Marooned!' The word 'marooned' is a lot of fun to say, especially in an evil roar. He added just one more for luck:

'MarooOoooOned!

You will never find her! Never! Marganulus Five is defeated! The time device is mine! And as soon as my laser arm is recharged, I shall use it to take complete control of history. Bwa-ha-haaaaa!'

'Hattie!' said Angus desperately. 'Isn't there anything you can do?'

'**I'm sorry,**' replied the voice of the computer. '**I can't help you at this *time.* I'd love to give you a *hand.* But any *minute,* Kragg is going to wreak havoc. He's really going to *tick* off a lot of people. So *watch* out.**' Angus screwed up his face in confusion. He'd never heard Hattie talk like this before. She'd been sarcastic and mocking, but right now it actually sounded like she'd gone a bit ***strange*** in her electronic brain.

'Hattie, are you trying to tell me something?' he said under his breath.

'**No, no. Absolutely not. *Bong!*' she replied. 'I haven't gone *cuckoo,* you know. I can't believe you haven't *clocked* what's going on yet.**'

'Proteus,' interrupted Kragg. 'How long until my weapon is ready?' During the night, Doctor Proteus had finally managed to weld together a makeshift charging cable for the cybernetic arm, which was now plugged into the wall. This is why Emperor Kragg was standing behind the door – he was unable to move more than two metres away from the nearest plug socket.

Doctor Proteus scuttled over and inspected a display on the underside of the robot arm. '***Thirty-eight minutes*** until full charge, Your Terribleness. And then, no part of history will be free from your control.'

'Excellent,' said Kragg, his eyes shining with greed – even the robot one. 'And, with Marganulus Five safely marooooooned in the past . . . there is nobody to stand in my way.'

'Oh, yes, there is!' said Akila.

'Who?' asked the evil emperor sharply.

'Well, erm. Me?' said Akila. 'Sorry, I thought that was obvious from my tone of voice. I'm going to stand in your way, you great hulking shouty robo-goon! And so is my friend! And so is McQueen!'

'**Woof!**' agreed McQueen. He had no idea what was going on, as he was a dog. But he had enjoyed hearing his name mentioned.

'Come on, Angus,' said Akila. 'Let's go! It's time to save the day!' Grabbing Angus by the hand, she pulled him to his feet and half-dragged him across the room towards the back door that led into the supermarket. Kragg tried to give chase but had forgotten that he was fastened to the wall by his charging cable. With a flash of sparks, he pulled the plug socket right out of the wall.

'Bahhh! Fix it, Proteus! ***Fix it!***' he cried.

'Don't you want to pursue the intruders, sir?' asked Proteus, who had started to chase Akila and Angus.

'Don't worry about the idiots! Let them go!' roared Kragg. 'What can they possibly do to stop me? Finish charging the weapon!' Proteus turned on his heel, allowing Angus, Akila and McQueen to wrench open the door and flee through the empty supermarket.

'What on earth are we going to do?' said Angus, panting as they ran. 'You heard Kragg – there's only just over half an hour to go until his laser cannon's charged. Then they're going to use the trolley to cause havoc right through history. Marge is trapped – and we don't know where! It's completely hopeless!'

Akila stopped and turned to face him. 'Think about it for a moment,' she told him. 'It doesn't matter how long it's going to take Kragg to charge up his laser. Half an hour, five minutes, ten seconds . . . It doesn't matter. Not if we've got a time machine!'

'Yes, but that's just it!' Angus stopped too, red-faced. 'We **don't** have a time machine! Kragg and Proteus have it!'

'Didn't you listen to Hattie?' Akila asked him, wide-eyed.

'Yes!' yelped Angus. 'She said she couldn't do anything! OK – she may have said it in quite a weird way, but . . .'

'She was giving us a clue,' Akila told him wearily. 'Think about it. What did she say? Something about *hands* . . . *minutes* . . . *tick* . . . *watch* . . . *time*? Doesn't that suggest anything to you?'

Angus tried to think. It's hard when you're panicking, and we're sorry to say that he didn't manage particularly well. He is the hero of this story, but we must warn you that the next thing he says is not particularly heroic or clever.

'***Buh?***' said Angus, scratching his head.

'She also said *clock!*' Akila stared at him, exasperated. 'She's giving us clues!' she yelled. 'Don't you remember? That news thing your mum and dad were watching? The clock tower in the town centre?'

Realization dawned over Angus's brain with the speed of a snail on a Sunday morning slither. 'The . . . clock tower?' he repeated, gaping at her. 'Oh, right . . . there's a shopping trolley up there, right?'

'Not just any shopping trolley,' she told him patiently. 'The actual Time Trolley. It must be!'

'But, but . . . how can it be up there? It's in Hyper-Buy!'

'You haven't got your head around this time-travel stuff, have you?' Akila began to lead him towards the front doors. 'If the trolley can journey through time, what's to stop Hattie sending it back to help us . . . from a time after this is all over. ***From the future!*** Get it now?'

'To be honest, no. Not really,' Angus replied, following her towards the doors. 'But I can't think of a better idea, so let's go!'

Angus and Akila raced into the town square, which was empty except for a few early risers hurrying to work and a couple of joggers. The stone structure of the town hall dominated the other side of the square, rising to a steeply sloping roof. In the middle, the tall clock tower cast a pointing shadow out across the cobbles. '***There it is***, ***look!***' said Akila, pointing. Shading his eyes from the morning sun, Angus squinted upward. Sure enough, stuck right on the top of the tower next to an elaborate weather vane in the shape of a cockerel, the silhouette of a shopping trolley could clearly be seen.

'Quick! There's no time to lose!' said Akila, rushing towards the front doors. 'Well,' she corrected herself, 'technically speaking, there is, because we are hopefully about to get access to a time machine. So, I suppose there isn't really any hurry. In fact, we could have stopped for breakfast. But never mind! Let's get going!'

'Are you ***absolutely sure*** that's the right trolley?' asked Angus, peering upward uncertainly.

'There's only one way to find out,' she told him. 'Come on!' One of the large double doors at the front of the hall was open, and a cleaner was visible inside, polishing the wooden floor with one of those spinny-roundy things that always look like they'd be fun to operate.

'Hall doesn't open till nine thirty!' he called to the pair of them as they dashed inside. 'And wipe your feet!' he added ineffectually. Ignoring him completely, they sprinted across the reception area to a wide staircase that rose from the back of the room, leaving a trail of dusty footprints. '***Typical***,' said the cleaner with a tut, steering his polisher towards the mess.

Akila led Angus further and further into the hall, dashing up staircases and along passageways, trying to find their way to the roof. 'I thought you said we didn't really need to be rushing,' gasped Angus, stopping to wipe the sweat from his brow. 'Couldn't we have a bit of a breather?'

'Not very ***dramatic***, is it?' asked Akila, beckoning to him. 'Whoever ambled on an adventure? If we're going to do this thing properly, we've got to hurry. Otherwise it's not a rescue mission. It's just . . . I don't know . . . a nice Sunday stroll.'

'Oh, all right,' he replied, taking a few deep breaths and following her along a narrow passageway right at the top of the main building. It was so near the roof that the ceiling actually sloped. At the end, there was an old wooden door with a key hanging on a hook beside it. Akila grabbed it and jabbed it into the keyhole with a rattle. 'How do you know how to use that?' asked Angus suspiciously. 'I thought a lock and key would be a bit ***high-tech*** for an Ancient Egyptian?'

'Don't be silly,' she told him.

FACT PIG

HI, KIDS! It's the Fact Pig here. Did you know that the Ancient Egyptians actually invented locks and keys thousands of years ago? They were used to seal up temples and tombs. And here's another really cool fact . . .

SHUT UP, FACT PIG, this is a very dramatic part of the story! Stop interrupting with history.

SORRY, oink.

Right, where were we? Ah, yes.

Behind the old door was a rickety wooden spiral staircase. From the dust on the treads it didn't look like anyone ever came up here, and cobwebs brushed their faces as they ***thundered*** up the creaky steps towards the top. Here, a very worn and warped wooden door led out on to the roof. The spiders' webs near it fluttered in the draughts that came through the leaky frame, and the filtered sunlight from outside made the dust dance and sparkle. 'I think this one's locked, too,' said Angus, trying the rattly old handle.

'Out of the way, future boy,' said Akila, moving him gently to one side. With an Ancient Egyptian battle cry, she aimed a ***high kick*** at the door, which burst outwards in a shower of wood chips. 'That's better,' she said, leading him out on to the roof.

'I thought you knew all about locks and keys?' mumbled Angus, following her.

'Sometimes there just isn't time,' his friend explained. 'Here it is, look!' Sure enough, as Angus stumbled out gingerly across the sloping tiles, he could see the Time Trolley balanced rather precariously on the apex, right beside the large white clock face. Or at least, it ***looked*** like the Time Trolley. Once again, the unpleasant thought struck him that it could simply be a perfectly normal shopping trolley that somebody had placed up here as a prank.

'Hattie,' he said urgently. 'Hattie, do you read me? Is this you? Or is this just your average everyday kind of shopping trolley?' There was no reply.

'Maybe it's run out of charge,' said Akila, joining him

and running a hand over the plastic handle at the back of the trolley. 'Perhaps Hattie won't activate until we start moving. Remember, the trolley needs kinetic energy to power up.'

'Start moving?' squawked Angus in alarm, looking over his shoulder. 'But if we start moving, we'll fall off the roof!'

'Yes,' explained Akila patiently. 'But when the trolley reaches eight miles an hour, we'll be able to time-jump. So we won't crash into the ground.'

'Unless, of course,' Angus pointed out, 'this isn't actually the Time Trolley. And it's just a shopping trolley that somebody stuck up here on the roof for a joke.'

'What's the joke?' she asked, looking puzzled.

'I dunno.' Angus waved his hands uncertainly. 'Trolley on a roof. It's just . . . ***funny***, isn't it? You know, it's out of place. Like, erm, I dunno . . . a dolphin on a roller coaster. Or a badger playing tennis.'

'What's a badger?'

'Doesn't matter,' said Angus. 'Just saying, you know. Things in unusual places are funny.'

'Well, if this is a shopping-trolley-on-the-roof joke,' said Akila, clambering in behind him, 'then we're not going to find it particularly funny. Instead, it's going to hurt – really quite a lot. Because instead of powering up and travelling through time, this trolley is simply going to plummet to the ground and land there in a pile of ***twisted metal***.' Angus peered ahead over the edge of the roof.

'I don't especially like the sound of that,' he said doubtfully.

'I don't like the sound of Emperor Kragg taking over time,' replied Akila. 'Come on. Let's do this.'

'Actually, I might have changed my mind . . .' began Angus, but it was too late. Akila reached out a leg behind them and kicked firmly against the weathervane. And the trolley began to rattle forward, rapidly gaining speed as it clanked across the roof tiles. With a sickening lurch, it careered over the edge and began to ***plunge*** towards the ground below.

CHAPTER 13

THE GREAT DUNGEON RESCUE

Here's a quick physics lesson for you. A shopping trolley with two children inside falls off a town-hall roof. The trolley must reach eight miles an hour in order to activate its onboard computer and travel through time.

QUESTION: does the trolley reach the required speed, or does it smash into the ground?
Please show all workings.

HI, KIDS! It's the **FACT PIG** again. Ooh, this sounds really fun and educational! I love sums! Shall we work this one out together?

NO, shut up, Fact Pig. We were just being silly. You're slowing the plot down again at a crucial and exciting stage. Go and have a wallow in the mud or something. Eat some potato peelings.

Ooooh, potato peelings. My favourite.

Yes, we know. Go on, off you trot.

Don't you want some help working out your fun physics homework?

No, that's fine. Go away.

OK, bye, guys! Enjoy the exciting climax to your time-travel story.

Yeah, cheers, Fact Pig. See you.

Will you be needing any further facts before the end of the story?

No, we've got this from here. That's fine, thanks. We didn't need any in the first place, to be honest.

Oh.

Fact Pig looks sad and walks off slowly while the audience all go 'aaah'

Right, he's gone. Where were we? Ah, yes.

The trolley ***careered*** over the edge of the town-hall roof and began to plunge towards the ground below. 'We must be going at eight miles an hour by now!' shrieked Angus in panic. 'Where's Hattie?'

'Maybe this is just an ordinary grocery chariot after all,' said Akila, looking pale with fright.

'Now you tell me!' The ground rushed up to meet them, looking flat and hard and very, very uncomfortable.

'**Time systems activated,**' said Hattie suddenly. '**Hello, you two. You solved my clever clues to the clock tower, then? *Impact in two seconds*, by the way. Did you want to time-jump away or crash into the floor?**'

'Time-jump! TIME-JUMP!'

shouted Akila and Angus in unison.

'Right you are,' replied the computer. And a split second before an impact that would have made this book require a warning sticker on the front, the trolley vanished with a *whoomf* and a flash of flame. Immediately, Angus and Akila were thrown backwards as it levelled off and began racing through the swirling purple light of the strange void between time called the chill-out zone.

'Where to, then, governor?' said Hattie. **'Hey, I'll tell you who I had in the back of my time machine the other day. Only that evil Emperor Kragg. *Right chatterbox*, he is.'**

'Where did he take Marge?' demanded Angus. 'He said he's marooned her in the past!'

'And then he repeated the word "marooned" several times,' added Akila. 'It was really weird.'

'**He shut her in a *dungeon*,**' the computer told them. '**Told her it would keep her out of mischief while he took control of the entire planet for all eternity.**'

'What dungeon?' demanded Angus. 'Can you take us there?'

'**Of course I can take you there,**' Hattie replied. '**I'm a hugely powerful time-travel computer. I can take you anywhere.**'

'OK, then,' said Angus. 'Will you take us there?'

'**That depends,**' Hattie told him.

'On what?' Angus wanted to know.

'**On whether you ask me to or not.**'

Angus gave a brief scream of frustration. 'Will you . . . ***PLEASE*** . . . take us to the dungeon where Marge is imprisoned? Please? Pretty please?'

'**Thought you'd never ask,**' said the computer. And there was a flash of bright sunlight as the trolley left the void and entered a new time zone.

'Which dungeon?' Angus wanted to know.

'**I'm not exactly sure which one,**' replied Hattie. '**But it's underneath that castle somewhere.**' Sure enough, visible below them was a gigantic medieval castle.

Colourful pennants fluttered on top of the pointed towers, and guards in armour could be seen patrolling the new-looking battlements. There was a blare of trumpets.

'Coolest thing ever,' said Angus, who had always loved castles.

'Don't see what's wrong with a nice pyramid, myself,' retorted Akila with a sniff. 'Very nice, pyramids.'

Hattie landed the trolley neatly in a small grove of trees not far from the main castle gates, where a wide wooden drawbridge led across the moat and into a large, bustling courtyard. '**Back here in *thirty minutes*, please,**' the computer warned them as they hurried away.

'It smells,' said Akila disapprovingly, wrinkling up her nose and kicking at a small heap of dirty straw as they crossed the courtyard. 'Ancient Egypt is far cleaner.'

'Focus,' Angus told her. 'We've got exactly half an hour, remember? We need to get in there –' he pointed to the tall castle keep – 'to free Marge from the dungeons and escape. Then make a plan to get back to my own time . . .'

'The Age of the Idiot?'

He winced. 'I really wish everyone would stop calling it that.'

Akila gave his arm a friendly squeeze. 'I don't think you're an idiot,' she told him.

'Thanks,' said Angus with a grin.

'It's just a shame that most of the other people living in your time are,' she added with a smile.

'Anyway . . .' Angus pointed to the closed door to the castle keep. 'Let's get this ***rescue mission*** underway, shall we?'

'Halt!' said one of the pair of guards flanking the heavy portcullis as they approached. 'What's your business here?'

'We've travelled through time to rescue our friend from the dungeon,' said Angus without thinking. Akila dug him sharply in the ribs.

'You what?' The guard leaned forward suspiciously.

'Nothing, nothing,' said Angus quickly.

'What my friend means,' added Akila smoothly, stepping in front of him, 'is that we've got an appointment.'

'You've got an ***appointment?***' The guard frowned. 'What sort of appointment?'

'We were told to report here, erm . . .' At that moment, a cockerel crowed loudly from the courtyard behind them. 'At the crow of that cockerel. To report to the, erm, you know . . .'

'To the kitchens?' asked the guard quizzically.

'The kitchens! **Yes!**' Akila agreed enthusiastically. 'That's it! We were told to report to the kitchens.'

'For we,' said Angus, stepping forward triumphantly, 'are the new kitchen hands!' He placed his hands on his hips in a dramatic, medieval kitchen-hand type of stance.

'New kitchen hands? We aren't expecting any new kitchen hands.'

'Well, you know what they say about ***kitchen hands***,' Akila told him confidently. 'They always arrive when you least expect them.'

'No, they don't,' argued the guard.

'They do,' Angus insisted. 'That's what they always say.'

'Norman!' the guard called to his opposite number, who was standing at the other side of

the doors. 'You ever heard anyone say that kitchen hands always arrive when you least expect 'em?'

'Yup.' Norman nodded sagely.

'Oh, well,' said the guard, stepping back. 'You'd better go in then. Kitchens are down the stairs on the right.' Scarcely believing their luck, Angus and Akila darted past him. The guard turned back to his colleague. 'Who did you hear say that, then?' he asked.

'That kid just there, a few seconds ago,' replied Norman. 'I heard him quite distinctly.' The first guard shook his head in frustration, looking over his shoulder into the main castle entrance hall. But, he reasoned, how much damage could two children really do in there? And if he raised the alarm, he'd have to admit he'd let them pass. He decided – wrongly – that it would be far safer just to let sleeping dogs lie.

The castle dungeons were wide, airy and spacious, with enormous picture windows looking out across sunlit gardens. No, not really. That wouldn't be very dungeon-like, would it? The castle dungeons were damp, dark and cramped. And they smelled really, really bad. *Nobody ever talks about the way history actually smells*, thought Angus to himself as, followed by Akila, he picked his way down a crooked, chilly stone staircase.

Hello! Greg and Chris here. Angus is right, isn't he? When was the last time your teacher told you anything about the way history ***smelled?*** But when you really think about it, it's quite important. As we've already discovered, Ancient Egypt smelled of hot stone and spices, with an undertone of camel droppings. Our own period, the Age of the Idiot, smells of petrol and bins, though we've all stopped noticing. And the dungeons of this medieval castle . . . well. How can we put this delicately? We can't. So we'll just have to give it to you straight. They smelled like the ***worst*** public toilets you've ever been in – and somebody filled one of the cubicles with rotten cabbages around a fortnight ago.

'Bleugh!' said Akila. 'This is ***revolting***. Worse than your time, Angus. Let's rescue Marge and get out of here.' They carried on descending the staircase, which was damp and slippery – it's best not to wonder why. At the bottom was a large guard room, with corridors leading off in two different directions towards the cells. And in the guard room, as you'd expect, was a guard. A very large and fairly dim guard. He sat comfortably at a wooden table with his hands laced behind his head and his sizeable belly sticking out from beneath his leather jerkin. On the table was a large bunch of keys.

'Right,' said Akila, peeping round the last curve of the staircase. 'Here's the plan. I'll distract the guard. You get the keys, let Marge out of her cell and meet me back here. Then we'll run away really, really fast.'

'How do we know which cell Marge is in?' whispered Angus.

'***MARGE?***' yelled Akila suddenly and very loudly. 'What cell are you in?'

'This one here,' came Marge's excited voice from the left-hand corridor.

'She's down there,' Akila told Angus, pointing. The

guard, meanwhile, had lumbered to his feet, alarmed by the shouting.

'Woss going on?' he said, squinting in the direction of the stairs.

'Meals for the prisoners!' called Akila brightly. Angus was, indeed, holding a tray that they'd managed to swipe while sneaking through the kitchens. But they hadn't been able to track down much food to put on it without being caught. So the wooden tray held nothing but a small, slightly shrivelled apple.

'It's apples today,' Angus told the guard, holding up the tray. 'Yum! Lovely apples.'

'It's not meal time,' said the guard suspiciously.

'That's because we're not really here to deliver meals,' said Akila cheekily, dashing past him and towards the right-hand dungeon entrance. 'We're here to call you a large, out-of-shape, silly-haired old ***bobble-nose***.' She stuck out her tongue and made an infuriating, high-pitched noise before disappearing down the passageway.

'Hey! Take that back! That's enormously hurtful, actually,' complained the guard furiously, lumbering after her.

Angus heard her voice echoing back from the dark stone walls. 'I'm doing a ***diversion!***' she cried.

'Yes, I worked that out for myself, thanks,' Angus replied, snatching the keys off the table and dashing in the other direction. Around halfway down the passageway, he could see a hand waving through the barred window in a cell door. 'Marge, is that you?' he called, running towards it.

'No,' said Marge sarcastically, 'it's Queen Catherine of Aragon. Who do you think it is? ***Of course it's me!*** Now, get this door open!'

'**Ten minutes to time jump**,' announced Hattie through his earpiece as Angus fumbled with the large bunch of keys. He found the right one on the seventh attempt, which was hugely frustrating, but we don't need to hold up the story by describing the whole process. Eventually the door swung open with a very castle-dungeony kind of a creak, and Marge stepped out into the corridor.

'Let's get out of here, shall we?' she suggested. 'It smells really, really appalling.'

'Yes, we've been through that,' Angus told her. 'Let's go! We've got a universe to save!'

'Slightly overdramatic, possibly,' said Marge, following him back towards the guard room, 'but yes, OK.' At that moment, Akila reappeared from the opposite archway, still making irritating noises.

'Quick! Up the stairs!' she said, catching sight of Angus and Marge. 'That guard is really, really annoyed with me. He's quite sensitive about his nose, apparently.'

'He has got kind of a bobbly nose, hasn't he?' agreed Marge.

'**OI!**' protested the guard, who was looming into view along the other dungeon passageway. At that point, everyone decided that Akila's suggestion of going up the stairs was an excellent and very timely one, and they clattered upward as fast as their legs could carry them. Which really was fairly fast.

Back at the front entrance to the castle keep, the two guards were still on watch and feeling slightly anxious about the two children they'd recently admitted. This anxiety did not diminish in the least when they heard a shout from behind them.

'***Stop those two children!***' bellowed the voice of the dungeon guard.

'I knew we shouldn't have let them in,' complained Norman, fumbling for his sword. 'I've been telling you for ten minutes now!'

'Shut up and get your sword out!' snapped the first guard. But before either of them could draw their weapons, Angus, Akila and Marge tore past them and dashed off across the courtyard. The jailer and both guards gave chase.

'They're gaining,' said Akila tersely, glancing over her shoulder. 'We need to slow them down. I don't fancy being ***kebabbed*** by one of those swords.' (She had learned about kebabs during her first week in our time and they had quickly become one of her favourite foods, along with fish fingers.) 'Quick!' she told Angus as they ran. 'Goose that horse!'

'Goose the horse?' Angus looked frantically to one side. Sure enough, a sleepy-looking horse was standing there, tethered to a cart full of turnips. 'What do you mean, goose the horse?'

'Goose it!' said Akila. '***Goose it good!*** You know, pinch its bottom! Oh, never mind.' With a tut, she ran towards the horse. 'I'll goose it myself.' And that's exactly what she did, giving the horse a firm tweak on its horsey behind. With a startled snort and an outraged neigh that sounded like it was saying '**Nooooo!**' the horse reared up and bolted forward, sending a tornado of turnips tumbling towards the terrified townsfolk. Angus heard a series of cries and **thumps** from behind as their pursuers tried, and failed, to run across the avalanche of vegetables. (We don't know if you've ever tried to run across an entire upset cartload of turnips, or indeed any kind of vegetable, but believe us, it's almost impossible without falling over. We tried it yesterday and Greg hurt his ankle quite badly.)

As they raced through the entranceway to the castle, Angus noticed a large wooden wheel across to one side. With a dim recollection of one of his history lessons, he glanced upward, to where the large metal portcullis was suspended above the main archway. 'Hang on a sec,' he told Akila, veering off to the side and **grabbing** the wooden lever. He gave it a sharp pull and immediately heard a clanking, as the wheel started to spin and the heavy portcullis began to drop. 'Go, go, go!' Angus told Akila and Marge, sprinting towards their rapidly closing

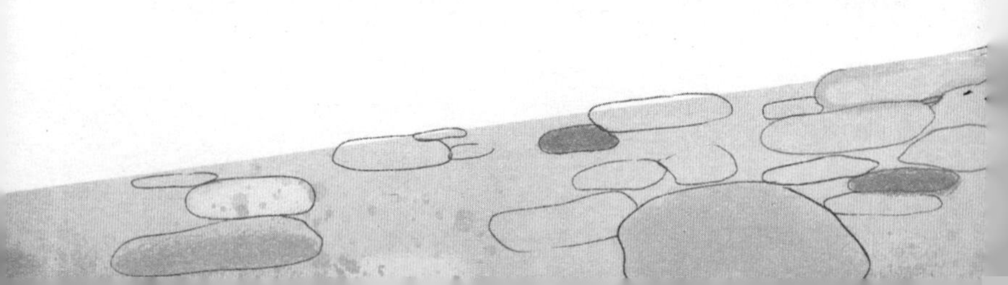

escape route. With seconds to go, it slammed down into the stone, impaling a stray turnip with a wet *splat*.

'That was almost your ***head***, future boy,' Akila told him. 'But I'm glad it wasn't. Come on!' Holding out a hand, she lifted him to his feet and they sprinted across the drawbridge towards the patch of trees where the Time Trolley was hidden. 'Ready to head back to the Age of the Idiot and stop Kragg's evil plans?' Akila asked Marge as they ran.

'Almost,' Marge told her. 'But I think we might need to make a few stop-offs on the way back. I can't face Kragg alone. We're going to need a bit of help.'

CHAPTER 14
SHOPPING FOR HEROES

A cold north wind swept spatters of icy spray up from the grey surface of the waves as the Viking longship steered towards the distant shore.

(Ooh, this is ***exciting***, isn't it? Why not imagine some cool music to go with it, probably involving a lot of drums and a horn going *taran-taraaa.*)

In the pointed prow of the boat, Bjorn Bloodclaw wrapped his fur-lined cloak tightly around himself and peered into the mist. 'Row, my friends!' he called to the oarsmen behind him. 'Row for your lives! We shall have a great battle this day! Battle and spoils! ***Onward to victory!***' The drum beat faster and the Vikings strained at their oars. Bjorn gripped the rail as the increased speed made the longship's prow rise out of the cold, dark sea.

'It's always got to be a **battle**, hasn't it?' muttered Edgar Smallspear to his neighbour on the third bench back. Edgar was a fairly reluctant Viking.

'What do you mean?' asked the man next to him, who was enormous, with arms like gnarled tree roots and a beard big enough to make even his fellow Vikings envious. And, as you can imagine, it was up against some fairly stiff competition in the beard stakes.

'Well, Thor Hugebeard,' replied Edgar, 'I just wonder whether there might be more to life, you know? I mean, we sail and row for ages in order to reach an Anglo-Saxon settlement or a monastery or something, then we just run about roaring and stabbing people and steal all their stuff. I mean, is that really all you want out of life?'

Thor Hugebeard looked at him blankly. 'I'm a Viking warrior,' he said matter-of-factly. 'You have just described in exact detail what a Viking warrior does. Why else would we come all this way? If we do some really impressive rampaging today, we might even end up in the *Anglo-Saxon Chronicle*. We'd be ***celebrities!***

Anyway, what do you want to do instead? Settle down and raise pigs?'

'I actually do,' said Edgar Smallspear. 'I've never told anyone this, but I'd love to pillage myself a nice plot of land somewhere in East Anglia. It's lovely and warm there, not like home. I could get myself a nice smallholding, maybe marry a nice Anglo-Saxon girl. Really integrate into the community, you know? Probably contribute to the development of its language and culture . . . that kind of thing.'

Thor Hugebeard was about to say something really scathing and Vikingy at this point, but he was interrupted by the scrunch of shingle as the longship grounded on a windswept beach and the Vikings all leapt out and pulled their craft away from the breakers. Bjorn Bloodclaw waited for a few moments, so as not to get his brand-new reindeer-fur boots wet, then leapt out on to the pebbles with a blood-curdling battle cry. '**BHAAARGHH!** Onward, my Vikings! Onward to victory! Today swords shall be shattered, bones shall be broken! Foes shall fear us, a fierce force!'

'He really does love a bit of alliteration, doesn't he?' muttered Edgar Smallspear.

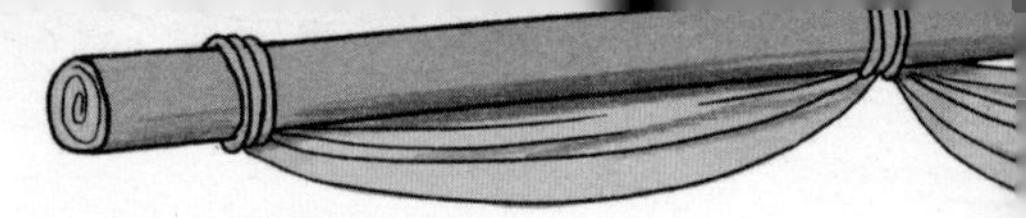

'Now for wrath!' continued Bloodclaw, drawing his sword and waving it around. 'Now for raging! Valhalla awaits! ***Oh*, *hello*, *Marge***. What are you doing here?' The Vikings turned to follow their leader's gaze. There, parked neatly on the beach not far away, was a strange metal device with two children sitting inside it. And, standing beside it was a smallish, smiling woman with curly hair.

'Who's that, then?' asked Smallspear.

'Dunno.' Thor Hugebeard pursed his lips thoughtfully. 'Must be one of the ***gods***, I suppose.'

'Oh, right.' Edgar nodded. 'Not Odin, though.'

Thor snorted contemptuously. 'Course it's not Odin,' he retorted. 'Count the **eyes**, you idiot.' While this intelligent discussion had been going on, Bjorn had marched over to join Marge, who handed him a translation earpiece.

'You come to barter for some more of that monk-made cheese?' he asked once the earpiece was in. 'Because you're too early. I haven't plundered any monasteries yet today. You'll have to wait for an hour or two.'

'Actually, Bloodclaw, dear, I was wondering whether you wouldn't mind giving me a hand with something quickly,' Marge told him with a winning smile. 'I need a bit of help dealing with a **monster**, you see.'

'A monster?' Bloodclaw's eyes gleamed fiercely. This sounded thrilling, just the exact sort of thing that Vikings used to really, really enjoy. *If it's a particularly terrifying monster*, he thought to himself, *they might even write a saga about me*. He'd always wanted to be in a **saga**. 'And where is this monster?' he asked excitedly.

'It's more a case of *when*, to be honest,' Marge began, before stopping herself. 'Well, never mind that,' she told the warrior. 'If you just jump into my, er, magic chariot here, it'll take us where we need to go. Don't touch that, dear.' Akila, looking fascinated, had clambered out of the trolley and was knocking her fist on the side of the longship.

'Sorry!' she called back. 'Just interested! This is bigger than my dad's boat. I like the dragon on the front.' The prow of the ship was indeed decorated with a fearsome carved dragon's head.

'Will we be voyaging to one of the other realms?' Bloodclaw wanted to know. 'Shall we take Bifröst, the rainbow bridge, to Jotunheim to battle a giant? Or must we brave Muspelheim, the fire kingdom?'

'Something like that,' Marge replied.

'Oh,' added Bloodclaw, his eyes glinting with an inner Viking light, 'I don't suppose you've got any of that ***Puppy Soft*** paper with you?' He shifted slightly uncomfortably inside his armour.

'I'll sort you out later,' Marge promised him. 'Now, hop in, and don't forget your sword. It won't take long, I promise. I'll have you back here before you can say "Beowulf".'

One sunny afternoon in Stratford-upon-Avon, Mr William Shakespeare was sitting in his front garden contemplating the flower beds.

'I wish you'd stop lounging about in the front garden and ***give me a hand!***' came an angry voice through the open front window of the cottage. 'What are you doing out there? Trying to work out how to spell your own surname again?'

'Who will tame this wretched shrew?' muttered Shakespeare to himself, adjusting his doublet.

'I heard that,' warned the voice. 'Now come and do some dusting, thou cream-faced loon.'

'Oh, that's rather good,' said the playwright, rummaging in his hose pocket for a piece of parchment. But just then there was a flash of light and a blast of hot wind. '**Gadzooks!**' exclaimed Shakespeare. 'What foul witchcraft is this? Oh, it's you, Marge. How now? Got any of that lovely Puppy Soft paper with you?' Sure enough, the Time Trolley had materialized beside him, giving off a cloud of smoke.

'What's that foul and pestilent congregation of vapours?' screeched the voice from inside the cottage. 'It'd better not be interfering with my roses.'

'Ah, thy roses,' began Shakespeare. 'That which we call a rose . . .'

'No time for blank verse now, dear,' Marge told him. 'I need your help.'

'***His help?***' retorted Anne Hathaway, who had now appeared at the window holding a duster. 'What help is he going to be? He hath no more brains than I have in my elbows!'

'Ooh, that's good too,' murmured Shakespeare. 'You really should write some of this stuff down, dear. Now, Marge, how can I assist you, my lady?'

'Well, we need to mount a daring rescue mission,' Marge explained, leaning to one side to reveal the other people sitting in the trolley behind her. 'This is Angus and Akila,' she explained. 'And this is Bjorn Bloodclaw, one of the fiercest warriors in history.'

'How now?' said Shakespeare politely to each of them.

'And I was rather hoping you might come along and give us a couple of ***rousing speeches***,' Marge went on. 'You know, provide a bit of moral support.'

'I'd be delighted,' he replied.

'Oh, I bet you would,' retorted his wife from the window. 'Anything to get out of helping with the chores, thou knotty-pated fool!'

'Sorry about her,' said Shakespeare with a sigh. 'She hath a February face. So full of frost, of storm, of cloudiness.'

'Well, maybe you should give her a hand with the housework every now and then,' Akila told him disapprovingly. 'You lot have got a load of catching up to do. Where I come from, we share the work equally.'

'And where might that be?' asked William Shakespeare, climbing awkwardly into the shopping trolley and settling himself awkwardly next to Bjorn Bloodclaw, who politely moved his large axe to give the playwright a bit more space.

'It's kind of a long story,' she told him honestly.

'Just one more stop to make before the climactic battle scene,' Marge told them. 'Hang on tight!'

'Are we going to add another ***fearsome warrior*** to our army?' asked Bjorn, his bright blue Viking eyes glittering hungrily.

'We certainly are,' Marge told him. 'One of the most fearsome warriors of all time. I think you'll like her.'

*

'Charging complete, Your Terribleness!' Doctor Proteus clapped his hands delightedly. He unplugged Emperor Kragg's robot arm from the makeshift charger that he had eventually constructed out of a selection of different Idiot Age cables.

'Excellent!' With an evil cackle, Kragg stood up, his head brushing the storeroom ceiling. 'At last, I am ready! ***At long, long last!***'

'It's only been thirty-seven minutes,' Proteus reminded him, looking wounded. Designing and building the new charger with what was, to him, prehistoric technology had actually been rather difficult and complicated. He'd been expecting a bit more praise for his speed rather than the hurtful phrase, 'At long, long last.' I mean, imagine if you'd cooked a really good meal for someone and when you walked in they went, 'Ah, dinner! At long, long last!' Thoughtless. But that's the thing with evil dictators, whatever time period they might come from. No manners.

'Silence!' roared Kragg, displaying a further lack of manners. He didn't even say, 'Silence, *please*.' 'Bring the time device out to the exterior of this primitive comestible-vending facility!' he went on. 'It is time to rampage through all of time, until everyone bows before me! **Bwah ha-ha-haaaa!**' Proteus obediently pushed the trolley towards the doors leading to the car park, which he had to open awkwardly by shoving them with his shoulders while holding the handle of the trolley with both arms. Kragg could easily have helped him but – as we've already discussed – he had no manners. You don't get to be an evil dictator from the far future by helping other people open doors. It really isn't in the supervillain playbook.

Because of Proteus's awkward door-opening position, he entered the car park backwards, so he didn't notice what was there waiting for them. Kragg didn't notice immediately because he was too busy going '**bwa-ha-ha**' in a variety of different ways. But when they did both notice, it stopped them in their tracks. Kragg's evil laughter dried up in his throat mid '**bwa**'. There, beneath the orange street light, stood Marge, with her hands on her hips in a dramatic 'not so fast' kind of pose. And behind her was a second, identical Time Trolley, jammed with people. In fact, it wasn't a second, identical Time Trolley. It was the exact same Time Trolley. (This is where the plot gets slightly confusing. But all will be explained. Just go with it for now, OK?)

'Not so fast, Kragg,' said Marge. 'I swore you'd never get your hands on my time machine. And I'm here to take it away from you. And when we get back to the ninety-ninth century, I'll have more than enough evidence to get you put away in prison for good.'

'You think you're going to stop me?' snarled Kragg. 'You and what army?'

'Ah, yes,' said Marge. 'I'm glad you mentioned my army. Allow me to introduce a few helpers who'll be assisting me in this evening's villain-defeating. This is Bjorn Bloodclaw – the most feared Viking warrior of the ninth century.'

'BLOOD!' bellowed Bjorn, leaping from the trolley and waving a large double-bladed axe above his head. 'BLOOD! BLOOD! BLOOD, BLOOD, BLOOD!' It was kind of his pre-battle catchphrase.

'**BLOOOOOOOOOD!**' he added for good measure, stamping his furry boots on the car park and baring his teeth.

'Thank you, Bjorn, dear. That's the spirit,' said Marge. 'Also with me is Mr William Shakespeare. He's not great at fighting but he can whip you up a sonnet quicker than you can compare something to a summer's day.'

'Ooh, that's a good one,' said Shakespeare, scrabbling for his quill.

'Why is this weak, ***strange-trousered*** fellow here, anyway?' Bjorn wanted to know. 'He cannot fight, you just said so yourself. *I* can fight,' he added. 'BLOOD!' He waved his axe again. (Vikings aren't great fans of the talky part before a battle. They like to get straight on with the hitting bits.)

'I thought it might be nice to have someone to take notes,' Marge explained. 'So we've got a nice souvenir afterwards. And also, he's great at rousing speeches, just in case we get a bit deflated at any point. Not that yelling "blood" isn't ***very useful***, Bjorn.' The Viking gave a satisfied smile. 'Then we've got Angus, joining us from the Age of the Idiot, and Akila representing Ancient Egypt,' Marge continued, turning back to Kragg. 'They're sort of the reason we're here in the first place, actually. I was trying to help Angus with his homework.'

'Hello,' said Angus with a meek wave.

'And also in the trolley,' finished Marge, 'we've got Emmeline Pankhurst – founder of the Suffragette movement and, something not a lot of people know, a martial arts expert.'*

'***HI-YA!***' screamed Emmeline Pankhurst dramatically, her long skirt swishing as she vaulted over the side of the trolley and took up an offensive stance.

* **FACT PIG NOTE**: this is actually a thing and is worth a Google.

'And don't forget McQueen,' Angus reminded her.

'**Woof**,' agreed McQueen.

And so the lines were drawn for the most incredible battle ever to take place in several different parts of history at the same time.

CHAPTER 15
MARGE'S TIME ARMY

So, here we are, ready for battle. A thrilling battle for control of time itself. It's all very exciting, so let's quickly remind ourselves of the teams before it all kicks off.

TEAM MARGE

- ***MARGE***, AKA Marganulus Five: Time-machine inventor from the ninety-ninth century and cheese enthusiast. Special abilities: large supply of jelly babies in trouser pocket.
- ***HATTIE***: Powerful onboard computer and translation engine. Special abilities: sarcasm.

- ***ANGUS***: Kid from the Age of the Idiot. Special abilities: making fish-finger sandwiches.
- ***AKILA***: Ancient Egyptian time traveller, rocks a braid and a scarf. Special abilities: can read and write hieroglyphs, which doesn't often come in useful in the current time period but is extremely cool.
- ***BJORN BLOODCLAW***: Viking warrior. Special abilities: hitting people with a large axe while shouting, 'BLOOD!'

- ***EMMELINE PANKHURST***: Campaigner for women's rights. Special abilities: low tolerance and martial arts, which is a great combination in this kind of situation.
- ***WILLIAM SHAKESPEARE***: Playwright, poet and official note-taker for this monumental battle. (A bit like the person who writes down what people say in court, only with more shouting and fighting.)
- ***McQUEEN***: Dog.

TEAM EQUIPMENT:

- Time-travelling shopping trolley.
- Axe, sword and other assorted Viking weapons.
- Parchment for Will to write his notes on. And a quill.

TEAM KRAGG

- ***EVIL EMPEROR KRAGG***: Supervillain from the ninety-ninth century. Plotting to take over the planet for all time and plunge the world into a never-ending era of darkness. He's the baddie, if that isn't clear by this point. Special abilities: hugely strong, massive, has evil cackle. Oh, and the laser arm. Did we mention the laser arm? He's got a laser arm.
- ***DOCTOR PROTEUS***: Genius scientist and snivelling sidekick. Special abilities: science and snivelling.

TEAM EQUIPMENT:

- The same time-travelling shopping trolley, only from a different point in its own timeline.
- And, if we forgot to mention this before, a laser arm.

Marge and her time army stood proudly in front of the trolley. Angus edged slightly closer to Akila, looking edgily at the gigantic form of Kragg.

'You really think you can stop me – the most powerful and most evil villain in all of history?' roared the evil emperor gloatingly. 'With this rag-tag bunch of misfits?'

'Oh dear, Marge,' sighed Emmeline Pankhurst. 'Yet another man who thinks the whole world revolves around him. Shall we teach him a lesson?' And it was at this point that the great time battle truly began. Because, without waiting for anyone to say 'charge' or something similar, Mrs Pankhurst darted forward and aimed a ***high kick*** directly at Kragg's knee. (Even though it was a high kick, he's eight feet tall, remember, so it didn't reach any higher.)

'YOW!' wailed evil Emperor Kragg. Even evil emperors dislike being kicked in the knee, especially with a pair of properly made sturdy Victorian hobnail boots. They have very tough and rather ***pointy*** toes (the boots, not the emperors). Emmeline Pankhurst followed up her high kick with a leg sweep that took the emperor's legs out from underneath him, and he was laid flat on his back with a very satisfying *clang* as his robot arm hit the tarmac. Our high-kicking suffragette hero returned to the Time Trolley, throwing in a backward somersault for good measure. (We're not sure whether the real Emmeline Pankhurst was actually able to do backward somersaults but it'll look **amazing** in the film.)

'Very nice, Emmeline,' Marge congratulated her. 'Now, Bjorn, if you'd like to tie him up and secure his little sidekick over there, we can stick him in the trolley and dump him back in the ninety-ninth century, where he can't do too much more harm. Well, he can do quite a bit of harm. But only in his own time – that's the main thing.'

Bjorn Bloodclaw hurried forward, waving his axe and throwing in a quick 'Blood!' for good measure. Shakespeare, deciding that the battle was nearly over, felt that this might be the moment for a bit of celebratory poetry.

'We few, we happy few,' he proclaimed loudly, standing up in the shopping trolley and holding a hand in the air, 'we ***band of brothers*** . . .'

'And sisters,' corrected Emmeline Pankhurst.

'Oh, yes, sorry, madam,' said Shakespeare. 'We band of brothers . . . and ***sisters***. Oh, you've spoiled my flow now. I've got too many syllables. Hang on.'

'Well, apologies if it spoils your poetry to include an entire half of the population,' said Emmeline archly.

'He doesn't help with the dusting, either,' chipped in Akila. By now, two things had happened. Firstly, Viking warrior Bjorn had reached Kragg. But, secondly, Kragg had managed to lift himself back up from the floor and had, crucially, remembered that his right arm was a super-powered ***laser cannon***. He activated it with a bright flash of red, obliterating Bloodclaw's upraised axe, which disappeared completely, leaving him holding only a short, smoking length of wood.

'That was my favourite axe!' wailed the Viking. 'I once hit Thor Bighelmet with that axe.'

Kragg, by this stage, was correcting his aim, pointing the smoking muzzle of his arm-cannon right at Bjorn's chest.

'**Get out of the way!**' shouted Angus, darting forward. 'He's got a gun!'

'What's a gun?' asked Bjorn Bloodclaw. But the smoking stump of wood had given him the approximate idea that, whatever weapon was fastened to Kragg's hand, he didn't want to get hit by it. Just as Angus reached him, he dived out of the way. Kragg's laser bolt passed inches above his head, hitting one of the car park's lamp posts. With a shower of sparks, the pole toppled over, falling in front of Marge's trolley.

'Quick, Proteus,' said Kragg, seeing his moment. 'To the time device! We can swiftly escape into another time period and leave these annoying irrelevancies far behind! **Bwa-ha-ha!**'

'Or in front,' Proteus pointed out, as they raced for their own trolley. As we discovered earlier, time travel plays havoc with your figures of speech. And if you have a pedantic sidekick, it can get really, really annoying.

'Yes, yes,' said Kragg impatiently as they climbed in. 'They are the past! I am the future! Now, activate the device! Begin my triumph!'

'**Time circuits activated,**' said the voice of Hattie as Kragg and Proteus's trolley began to clatter forward and down the steep slope of the car park. '**Oh, hello,**' the computer added. '**There seems to be another one of me over there.**'

'**That's the problem with time travel,**' confirmed the version of Hattie in Marge's trolley. '**You never quite know when you're going to run into yourself. You're looking lovely today, by the way.**'

'**Why, thank you,**' Hattie told herself. '**And may I say that you are incredibly clever and quite the most brilliant computer ever invented.**'

'***Back to the trolley!***' called Marge to her team. 'We mustn't let them get away!' Bloodclaw and Angus raced back to join the others, piling into their own trolley as Kragg and Proteus rattled past. Their version of the Time Trolley was already building up speed, sparks shooting down the metal sides as it approached the eight miles an hour it needed to jump through time.

But before leaping in to join the others, Bjorn gave their trolley a long push that brought them closer to Kragg.

'We've got to stop him!' Marge yelled. '***Slow him down***, somebody!' With one last shove on the handle, Bjorn dived headfirst into the trolley, breaking Shakespeare's best quill in the process.

'How can we slow him down?' Angus asked Akila, looking in alarm at Kragg's trolley. Thanks to Bjorn's pushing, it was only a metre or so away. Both time machines were rapidly gaining speed as they rolled down the steep car park towards the brick wall at the bottom.

'Set the time circuits!' Kragg was roaring. 'They'll never be able to catch us!'

'I think I've had an ***idea***,' Akila told Angus suddenly, the long stripy woollen scarf around her neck billowing out behind her in a very dramatic fashion. Working quickly, she unwound the scarf from her neck and passed one end of it to Angus. 'Tie this to the front of the trolley,' she told him. 'Quickly!'

'It's a race against time!' said Angus breathlessly as he knotted.

'And it's a race *through* time,' Akila added.

'What are you going to do?' asked Angus.

'Tie the other end to their trolley,' she replied. 'Then we'll be able to follow them wherever they go.'

'Tie the other end to **their** trolley?' Angus squawked in alarm. 'How on earth are you going to do that?'

'Like this,' she shouted over the rattling of the trolley wheels. And, grasping the other end of the scarf tightly in one hand, she climbed up on to the edge of the trolley and took a gigantic leap towards Kragg and Proteus.

'That's my kind of girl,' said Emmeline Pankhurst proudly.

Kragg, unfortunately, had seen Akila preparing for her leap. He skewed round in his own time machine, aiming his laser arm at her. But, luckily, his bulk made it hard for him to turn fully and he was at an awkward angle when he fired. His laser blast actually went between Akila's legs as she ***vaulted*** high into the air and landed squarely on the back of Kragg's trolley, which was now covered with bright sparks as it prepared to jump through time. Quickly and deftly she knotted the scarf around the trolley's handle.

'Who knew a ***scarf*** would ever be useful for time travelling?' she yelled with a wink. 'There,' she added. 'That's a win for Ancient Egypt.'

'**Ancient Egypt, next stop,**' replied Hattie. '**You've got it.**' The trouble with having a powerful time-travelling computer listening to your every word is that it's sometimes hard to mention a period of history without her ***assuming*** you immediately want to go there.

'This is all very exciting,' said Shakespeare from the back of Angus's trolley.

'Sounds like he might have a speech coming on,' said Marge grimly.

'And gentlemen in England now abed,' began Shakespeare, 'shall feel themselves

accursed they were not here. And hold their manhoods cheap . . .'

'Gentlemen *and ladies*,' said Akila and Emmeline Pankhurst at the same time.

'Oh, gadzooks,' said Shakespeare. But, before he could correct his dramatic monologue, there was a blinding flash of light and both trolleys vanished, leaving twin sets of flaming tyre marks running down an empty, darkened supermarket car park.

CHAPTER 16

THE CHEESE CHARIOT

'Well, good morning, everyone, and welcome to the Thonis Arena for this afternoon's very exciting chariot race!' shouted the announcer. 'Here with me in the commentary gantry is my good friend Omari. And we're expecting an exciting race!'

'Good afternoon, Chiops. Good afternoon, everybody!' yelled Omari so the large crowd could hear him. 'And, yes, as the setting sun shines off the surface of the Nile, we are indeed about to witness a very, very thrilling contest. And thanks to whoever sent this ***lovely*** dish of dates to us here on the commentary gantry.'

'I think I can see the riders getting ready down there,' said his friend, peering into a large staging area at the beginning of the course. 'Most of the chariots seem to be ready. Just a few spare horses to be cleared away and I think we'll be ready to begin.'

HISTORICAL ASIDE FROM THE AUTHORS:

Did Ancient Egyptians have chariot races? Yes, they definitely did. Did they have ***commentators*** who spoke like modern-day sports broadcasters? Almost certainly not. But we thought it was funny. And this story has a time-travelling shopping trolley in it, so it's not like it's one hundred per cent historically accurate. Sometimes you've just got to go with it, ***OK?***

'And, what in the name of Nemty the falcon-headed god is going on down there?' continued the chariot-race commentator. 'I can see that one . . . no, two! Two ***very strange-looking*** chariots have appeared to join the race. It almost seemed as if they came out of nowhere. I can see three people in the first . . . yes, the servants are attaching a horse to it right now. And in the second, a whole load of chariot drivers.

There seem to be one, two . . . no fewer than five of them! And is that a dog as well? You don't see too many of those! And it looks like, yes, they're also being hitched up to a horse!'

'So, a couple of wild-card entries into this race, right at the last minute!' said Chiops excitedly. 'That's going to add an extra layer of tension to what is already a very hotly contested Nile Mile. It looks like they're under starter's orders . . .'

'And it's torches out, and ***away they go!*** ' added Omari, as a fanfare sounded and the chariots began to race through the enormous stadium. 'Looks like most of the chariots today have opted for the sandy-weather tyres. Though those two late entries seem to have rather strange, small wheels. And, oh my goodness! They've veered right out of the stadium! What in the world is going on down there?'

What was going on down there was this:

Both Time Trolleys had popped out of the void at exactly the same moment, landing neatly in the area where the chariots were getting ready to race. As they skidded to a rapid halt in the soft sand, Akila leapt out of Kragg's trolley, untying her scarf from the back and darting out of sight into the crowd.

'We need to get away from them, quickly!' Kragg roared at Proteus. 'Find a way to get us to ***eight miles an hour!*** We must escape through time as quickly as possible!'

Proteus thought fast. All around them, chariots were being fastened to horses in preparation for the race. 'You!' he yelled at one of the grooms. 'Attach some of those primitive animals to the front of my chariot! Quickly!' With a shrug, the groom gathered the leather harnesses of two horses and passed them to Proteus, who tied them to the front of the trolley, grasping the reins uncertainly at the same time.

Akila, meanwhile, was weaving back towards Marge's trolley, which had come to rest a little way away. Unlike Proteus, she was very familiar with Ancient Egyptian chariot racing, being an actual Ancient Egyptian. As she ran, she was already selecting from among the spare horses. 'Quick, my friend!' she shouted to one of the other grooms. 'Help me with this horse! No, not that one, that brown one! He looks faster! Hurry, hurry!' Throwing a look back over her shoulder, she could see that Kragg and Proteus already had two horses securely fastened to the front of their own trolley and were preparing to escape in among the hurly-burly of the race starting.

'Tie these on!' shouted Akila to Bjorn Bloodclaw, vaulting into the trolley with a selection of leather reins clutched in her hand. Bloodclaw, being a Viking sailor and quite good at knots, fastened the horse to their own trolley. The scene was now set for a dramatic Ancient Egyptian chariot race between two shopping trolleys. And that's not a sentence you hear every day.

'***Hyaa!***' The three torches at the start line were extinguished one by one, and with a cracking of whips and a clattering and scrunching of wheels on compacted sand, the chariots began to surge forward. Proteus flicked his reins uncertainly but the horses, trained to race, were already breaking into a trot. Kragg looked back over his shoulder with a leer of triumph as his trolley began to pull away.

'After them!' ordered Marge. 'If they reach eight miles an hour and time-jump, we'll have no way of knowing where they went!'

'I'll drive, if you don't mind,' Akila told Bloodclaw, taking the reins from his hands and flicking them expertly.

'Quite right, too,' Emmeline Pankhurst agreed.

'Ride on, ***thou noble trolley***, like the wind,' cried Shakespeare, standing up in the back and placing a hand on his chest. 'And run that evil emperor to ground! For when he doth captured be, verily, we shalt . . . what are we actually going to do to him?'

'Skewer him like a ***plump roasted reindeer!***' replied Bjorn with a bloodthirsty grin. Shakespeare looked rather shocked at this.

'We most certainly are not,' Marge told him. 'We're going to take him back to his own time and tip off the police that he's a complete wrong 'un.'

'That's not technically a crime,' Angus pointed out.

'It is in the ***ninety-ninth century***,' Marge reassured him. 'And it carries a sentence of not being allowed to do evil stuff for life. Justice has come on a long way since the Age of the Idiot, you know.'

'Can't I skewer him just a little bit?' pleaded the Viking. 'Just in the leg, maybe? Or bite one of his fingers?'

'Kicking him in the knee was extremely satisfying, I must say,' mused Emmeline Pankhurst, dusting her hands together.

'No kicking, and no skewering,' said Marge firmly. 'Well,' she relented, 'perhaps just a little bit of kicking.'

'***Huzzah!***' chipped in Shakespeare from the back. 'Lady Akila,' he pointed out, '***take heed!*** Thy quarry hath taken a sharp turn to the left, in an attempt to throw thee off the scent!'

Akila peered through the cloud of sandy dust kicked up by the chariots in front. Sure enough, Kragg and Proteus had steered away from the main pack, heading for one of the large archways leading out of the chariot arena.

'Hang on,' she told the others, pulling sharply on one of the reins. With a startled whinny, their horse plunged to the left, sending the trolley up on to two wheels as it made a sharp turn and headed off in pursuit. The crowd that had gathered in the arena gasped and applauded. They'd been hoping to see an exciting race. None of them could possibly have realized, however, that they would end up watching William Shakespeare, Emmeline Pankhurst and a Viking chasing a ***half-robotic cyborg villain*** from the ninety-ninth century. To be honest, even if it had been written on the poster they wouldn't have believed it.

Proteus shook the reins and urged his horses on, steering his trolley away from the racetrack entirely and out into the busy streets. Startled Egyptians leapt out of the way and pressed themselves against the brightly painted walls as it ***thundered*** down the narrow alleyways and roads between the high buildings, rattling and neighing echoing back from the stone. Akila expertly steered her own trolley in pursuit, shouting encouragement to their horses. Shakespeare, in turn, shouted encouragement to her from the back, where he was still standing and looking around him in wonder. 'This would all make a wonderful setting for a play,' he said to himself at one point.

After a while, Kragg's trolley burst out into a wide market square, and Akila took her chance. Steering her trolley alongside, she skilfully brought the two speeding chariots close together, sparks shooting from their wheels as they collided. '***Now***, ***Bjorn!***' she shouted. The Viking had been ready, crouched on the edge of the trolley in preparation for a great spring. He leapt across the gap between the trolleys, landing right next to Kragg, and began to wrestle the emperor, whose trolley veered wildly off course as Proteus let go of the reins to deal with this new threat.

'Watch out for that laser!' warned Angus, seeing Kragg lift his robotic arm. Bloodclaw ducked, but only just in time. A ***blast*** of bright energy shot right above his head, knocking the nose off a large statue that stood at the side of the square.

'That was close!' Bjorn yelled to Angus, grinning fiercely. 'Nearly bought myself a one-way ticket to Valhalla then!' Angus smiled weakly in reply.

'I think we need some **weapons** of our own,' decided Marge. 'Akila, look there! At the side of the square! Take us over there!' The girl peered in the direction Marge was pointing.

'Can't see anything there except a cheese stall!' she shouted.

'Exactly! Go, quick!' said Marge. 'We need weapons! Stinky ones! Cheese grenades, to be exact!' As they swept along the front of the stall, she leaned out and swept up several of the small, round pots of camel cheese.

'That stuff really, really smells,' remembered Angus.

'Exactly!' Marge tossed him one of the pots with a grin. 'Ready . . . aim . . . chuck the cheese!' Drawing her hand back, she launched her own pot in a powerful throw. It traced a graceful arc in the air and **smashed** right on the side of Kragg's head. Sloppy white cheese dripped across his ear and into his robotic eye, which sparked alarmingly.

'Argh! Chemical warfare!' He snarled furiously. 'What is this **noxious** prehistoric substance? It's interfering with my cybernetic systems. And it smells revolting!'

'It appears to be some form of primitive dairy product, Your Stinkiness,' said Proteus, dipping a finger in the goo and licking it thoughtfully. 'Ooh,' he exclaimed, 'it tastes nicer than it smells, actually.' But he was silenced when another pot, thrown by Angus, hit him directly on the top of the head, drenching his hair in camel cheese.

'***Bull's eye!***' yelled Angus.

'It's camel, actually,' corrected Marge, who was enjoying herself tremendously.

'Camel's eye, then,' said Angus. 'And here's another one!' He chucked a second cheese grenade, which smashed on the side of Kragg's trolley. By now, Akila had steered closer to them again, and Bjorn managed to leap back on to his own trolley just as Kragg aimed his laser arm once again. 'Look out!' cried Marge, as he levelled the weapon directly at them. Akila looked across in panic. There wasn't time to steer away.

'Jump!' she told the others. 'Jump ... ***NOW!***' Frantically, they all leapt from the trolley, rolling over and over on the warm sand as they landed. They were only just in time. Narrowing his eyes in evil triumph, Kragg launched a laser bolt directly at their Time Trolley. With a gigantic explosion, it disappeared, leaving nothing behind except a few fragments of hot, twisted metal and two ***very startled*** horses which – you'll be relieved to hear – were not hurt at all and retired to a nice farm shortly after the end of this story. But the Time Trolley had been completely destroyed.

CHAPTER 17

KRAGG TO THE FUTURE

Angus rolled over in the sand to join Akila, who was lying nearby. She placed a protective arm over him, squinting back across the square to the smoking pile of metal which had, until a few seconds ago, been the Time Trolley. 'I, er, I think your time machine just got a bit obliterated,' she told him.

As the reality hit him, Angus gave an ***alarmed*** noise that sounded not unlike a seagull having its foot trodden on. McQueen, who for once didn't seem to feel like escaping, scampered over with a whimper and nestled into the crook of his arm. 'Marge!' said Angus. 'The trolley's been destroyed! We're stranded in history!'

'I thought you were starting to like history,' she replied, getting to her feet a little unsteadily. Behind her, he could see Emmeline Pankhurst helping Bjorn Bloodclaw up. Nearby, Shakespeare was shaking sand out of his beard.

'I mean, I was getting ***interested*** in history,' he reasoned, 'but that doesn't mean I want to spend the rest of my life in it!'

'Oh, it's not so bad,' Akila told him, giving him a squeeze. 'I'll take care of you.' And Angus, despite the prospect of being trapped thousands of years in the past, felt a little better.

'Besides,' added Marge, 'don't give up yet. It's not over till it's over.'

'It's over,' said Angus, pointing behind her with a shaking finger. Stepping out of his own trolley and casting a gigantic shadow on the hot sand, the evil Emperor Kragg was stalking across the square towards Marge and her friends, his laser arm outstretched and a leer of triumph spreading across his face. 'So,' he spat, 'you really thought you could stand a chance against me? The ***greatest warlord*** that this planet will ever know? You puny worms!'

'Puny worms, ha-ha,' said Proteus, cringing along behind him. 'Very good. Puny worms. That's exactly what they are.'

'Shut up, Proteus,' snapped Kragg.

'Absolutely right, Your Nastiness,' said Proteus, taking a couple of steps back. 'That's me told. Very good.'

Kragg loomed over Marge. 'Marganulus Five,' he gloated. 'You lose. You had the entire course of human history, present and future, at your fingertips. And you still lost to me, Kragg! The all-knowing, all-powerful. And shortly . . . the **master** of time! And for you . . . well, I'm sorry to say that **your** time . . . is up. ***Bwa-ha-ha-haaaa***.'

'Yes, well . . .' Marge looked up calmly, directly into the muzzle of the laser cannon. 'That's all very lovely. But there might be one thing you've failed to take into account.'

Kragg frowned. 'What could I possibly have failed to take into account?' he snarled.

'Well,' said Marge. 'You think you're about to shoot me, right?'

'I *am* about to shoot you,' said Kragg.

'Well, if that's the case,' said Marge, 'then how come I'm alive in the future, and I'm standing right behind you?'

'***What?***' said Kragg, spinning on the spot. Sure enough, standing not far away in the Ancient Egyptian plaza was another Marge. And what was even more interesting was that she was sitting inside another Time Trolley. But this Marge, and indeed this Time Trolley, were a little different to the ones we've been getting used to so far. Here's how:

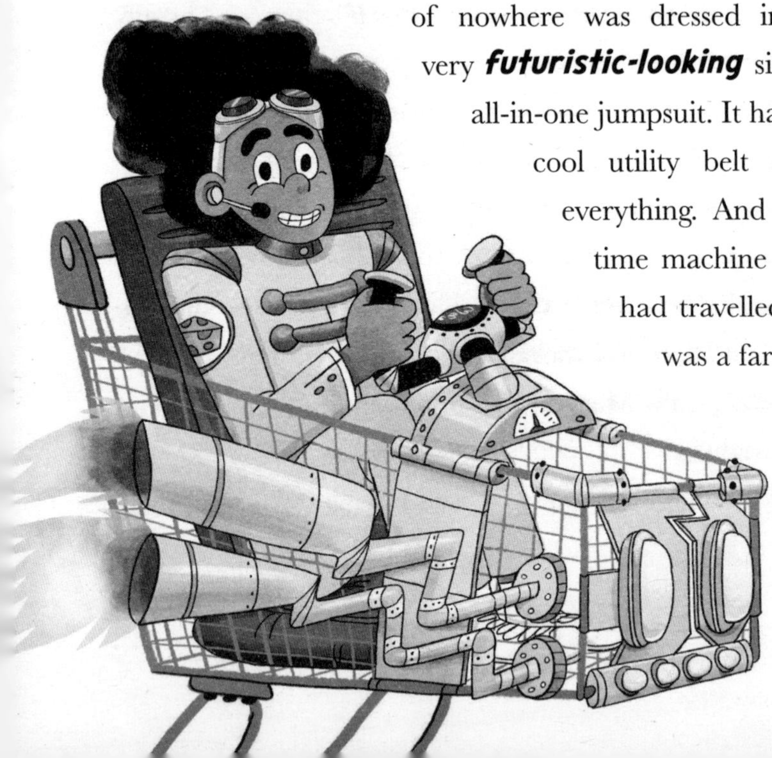

The new Marge who had suddenly appeared out of nowhere was dressed in a very ***futuristic-looking*** silver all-in-one jumpsuit. It had a cool utility belt and everything. And the time machine she had travelled in was a far cry from the rather rickety old shopping trolley with a wonky wheel. It was slick and state-of-the art. Its highly polished metal gleamed in the sun, and instead of small plastic wheels it had large ones with proper tyres. A flashing control panel was fastened to the handle at the back, and coloured lights strobed along the mesh at the front. It was, to put it simply, the ***coolest*** shopping trolley you have ever seen. In fact, the chances are you've never seen a shopping trolley that was even a little bit cool. But you know what we mean.

'***Oo-ooh!***' called out futuristic-jumpsuit-wearing Marge, giving a friendly wave. 'How is everybody? Lovely to see you all. Thanks so much for having me!'

'Looks like I decided to soup the old girl up a bit, doesn't it?' said the other Marge. 'Looking good, Hattie!'

'**Thanks!**' replied the voice of the computer from the high-tech trolley. '**You're right, this is the *new improved* Time Trolley! Much better than the previous version. It's been invented by you in the future, and I've brought it back to rescue you!**'

'Isn't this fun?' added future Marge, her silver suit glittering in the sunlight of Ancient Egypt.

PLOT UPDATE! We know time-travel stories can be a bit difficult to follow. So, to save you flicking back a few pages, here's a quick summary.

Kragg and Proteus travelled back to Ancient Egypt in the Time Trolley, and Marge and her friends followed in another version of the same trolley, which was then ***destroyed***. Now this future trolley has appeared. So how many shopping trolleys are in Ancient Egypt at this point? ***Two!*** Kragg's original trolley, and the new souped-up one. You just never know where a shopping trolley's going to appear, do you? They turn up in the most unexpected places. Anyway, is that all clear? Back to the story.

Evil Emperor Kragg had turned to face the new, shiny Time Trolley. And he broke into his largest evil cackle yet, only pausing briefly when a bit of camel cheese dripped down his cheek and went into his mouth. He gagged slightly – it really is an acquired taste. 'You fool, Marganulus Five!' he bellowed. 'You have invented an even better time machine and brought it back here to me? You must be ***even more stupid*** than I thought! I will simply take control of the new time device and become even more powerful! ***Bwa-ha-haaaaaa***.'

Behind him, original Marge had backed up to stand next to Angus. 'He's right, you know,' she said, looking thoughtful. 'That does seem like a bit of a dumb move. Why would I invent a nice shiny new Time Trolley and bring it straight to Kragg, looking like I'm dressed in tin foil. Unless . . . aha!' She snapped her fingers. 'I think I know what my plan is. Or rather, what it's going to be.'

'I have literally no idea what's going on,' replied Angus honestly.

'I think you're creating a diversion,' said Akila suddenly.

'I think you're right,' said Marge. 'OK –' she turned to the two of them – 'whatever happens, you need to capture Kragg and bring him back to Hyper-Buy, OK? ***Whatever happens***,' she repeated, looking each of them seriously in the eye.

'OK,' said Angus nervously.

'Bloodclaw and Emmeline are more than a match for him,' Marge went on, 'as long as you all attack while he's distracted. Now . . . *go*!'

'But where are *you* going?' said Angus, feeling panic about to overwhelm him.

'I'm grabbing his trolley while he's distracted, of course,' said Marge. 'Look, it'll all become clear. Just whatever happens, get Kragg back to Hyper-Buy.' And she sprinted off towards Kragg's now-empty Time Trolley, which was still attached to two horses, let's not forget.

'You heard her,' Akila told Angus. 'We need to help future Marge and keep Kragg distracted! Bjorn, Emmeline . . . **CHARGE!**' And, with the two warriors beside her, she dashed towards Kragg, who was advancing on the high-tech Time Trolley, his laser arm emitting a high-pitched whining as it recharged, ready to fire at future Marge, who was watching him calmly. But before he reached her, Bjorn Bloodclaw leapt on to his back from behind with a Viking war cry and started hacking at the robot arm with an axe. (His main axe, you may remember, was destroyed in the last chapter but this was a spare axe he kept in his boot. No self-respecting Viking would ever leave his longhouse without at least three axes.) Within seconds, Bloodclaw had cut through several thick wires, and the robot arm began to whirl out of control, shooting off small blasts of laser energy at random.

'I'm not sure that's exactly the outcome he was aiming for, do you?' said Akila to Angus, picking him up off the floor and taking shelter behind a market stall. Explosions echoed through the square and people began to flee in panic.

'***Aiyeee!***' wailed a smartly dressed Egyptian as he dashed past with the end of his robe on fire. 'Who IS that?'

'Probably one of the gods,' reasoned his friend, sprinting after him.

Original Marge, meanwhile, had reached the original Time Trolley. Luckily, Kragg was too distracted by the Viking hanging off his arm to notice this. And, more luckily still, she just managed to climb in before he started shooting laser blasts across the square. The horses, understandably, ***bolted*** in panic at this point. Marge managed to grab the reins

and Angus watched as her trolley careened across the plaza. Just before reaching the archway at the side it must have reached eight miles an hour because it disappeared, leaving the startled horses to run on alone. 'I wonder where she's gone,' he mused.

'I expect we'll find out,' Akila told him. 'Or maybe we've found out ***already***,' she added, 'but we haven't worked it out yet.'

'Time travel messes with my head,' complained Angus. Peeking out from behind the market stall, he could see that Bloodclaw was in danger of being shaken off Kragg's arm.

PLOT UPDATE! How many Time Trolleys are now in Ancient Egypt? ***Just one!*** The futuristic one with the cool wheels and the coloured lights. Who's going to get control of it? It's exciting this, isn't it?

'Oh, honestly,' said Emmeline Pankhurst, who had been watching the battle disapprovingly with her hands on her hips. Picking up her long skirt, she strode towards Kragg, who was still wheeling in a circle with Bloodclaw clamped to him. 'If you want something done properly, never send a man to do it. Especially not one with horns on his hat.' And with a giant kung-fu kick, she launched herself at the robot arm and clung on, kicking out at one of its control panels and shouting: 'Votes for women!'

'I'm an evil dictator,' Kragg pointed out. 'Technically I don't believe in votes for ***anybody***.'

'Sorry,' said Emmeline. 'Force of habit. Now, where was I? Ah, yes,' and she continued kicking frantically at the robot arm, as Kragg whirled in a circle trying to shake the Viking off his back.

Shakespeare was enjoying all this enormously. 'Kick, noble Pankhurst, kick the arm!' he declaimed, popping up from behind a statue. 'And bring this foul dictator to his knees! For, verily, he is a naughty knave . . . whose robot arm . . .

FLEEAAAAARGGH!'*

---

* William Shakespeare is credited with inventing many of the words which we use in the English language today. For example, *bandit*, *dwindle*, *lonely* and *fleeaaaarggh*. These

Kragg's laser arm had gone off just as he was facing in the playwright's direction. A bolt of energy shot out of the end, and Shakespeare only just ducked back behind his statue in time. The laser blast passed right over the top of his head, though, completely **obliterating** his hair except for two patches on either side, just above the ears. The top of his head was left completely bald. Unfortunately for him, his most famous portrait was painted the week after this story takes place.

'Ah,' said Angus, snapping his fingers. 'I knew he looked weird somehow. That's more like the Shakespeare I've seen in pictures.'

'Ah, well,' said Shakespeare philosophically, passing a hand over the top of his head. 'There's many a man has more hair than wit, I suppose.' Kragg continued rotating,

---

words mean 1) an outlaw, 2) to decline, 3) solitary and 4) 'Help! An evil dictator has just almost shot my head off.'

still firing off laser blasts at intervals. And now he had spun round to look directly at **future Marge**, who was still standing calmly beside the souped-up Time Trolley in her silver jumpsuit.

At the very last second, Angus realized what was about to happen. He saw Kragg's laser arm point directly at Marge. He saw her give a large, genuine smile.

'Thanks so much,' said Marge. 'I've had an absolutely lovely time.'

'**NOOOOOOOOO!**' howled Angus. McQueen, cowering at his feet, gave an anguished howl of his own. But it was too late. A bright bolt of laser energy shot out of Kragg's arm. For a split-second Angus saw its yellow light reflected from her silvery jumpsuit. Then Marge completely vanished in a flash of fire.

CHAPTER 18

KRAGG'S TRIUMPH

'NOOOOOOO!' wailed Angus again, feeling Akila's arm round his shoulder.

'Come on!' she told him. 'She did this for us! To create a distraction! Don't let it be for nothing! We need to get to that time machine! Now!' Numbly, he followed as she began to lead him out from behind the market stall and across the square.

Kragg, in the meantime, seemed to have surprised himself with his victory. He was silent for a moment, and then his evil cackle began to fill the plaza. 'I have defeated her!' he roared. 'Marganulus Five is no more! There is **nobody** to stand in my way!' Unfortunately he had forgotten in his moment of triumph that he still had a suffragette and a Viking clinging on to him, and he had just obliterated their friend.

'Well, now you've got me ***really***, ***really*** angry!' screamed Emmeline Pankhurst, kicking out at the robot arm with renewed fury. She managed to land a particularly hard blow with the heel of her high boot, right on a cluster of controls near the elbow. There was a huge bang and a rain of sparks, followed by a loud, descending hum. Kragg's glowing red eye went out.

'By Georgina, she's done it!' yelled Shakespeare, snapping out of a shocked silence during which he had been silently composing a very moving sonnet about Marge. At the same moment he noticed Doctor Proteus sneaking towards the Time Trolley. 'Oh no, thou dost not,' yelled the playwright (which is the Elizabethan equivalent of 'oh no, you don't'). 'Be thou not so hasty!' ('not so fast') he added and, grabbing his sharpest quill from the pocket of his doublet, he ***rugby-tackled*** Proteus to the ground and jabbed at him with it.

'Look, Angus!' he yelled, grinning. 'The pen is mightier than the sword!'

Angus replied with a thumbs-up.

'Ow! Stop it! I surrender!' squeaked Proteus as the sharpened feather jabbed into his arm.

'We've disabled his electrical systems!' shouted Emmeline Pankhurst at the same time. 'Just the outdated electoral system to go! Bloodclaw! Bring him down! Go for the legs!' And the Viking, dropping from Kragg's back, ***clamped*** his strong arms round Kragg's gigantic, thick boots. Slowly, like a great tree falling, Kragg toppled to the ground, his head glancing off a fallen statue that neatly knocked him out cold.

'We need to tie them up! Quick!' said Emmeline Pankhurst.

'Wait a second,' Akila replied. 'I'll just pop to Keket's Rope Stall over there. Best rope in the city.' In less than a minute she was back with a coil of soft, strong rope, and within another minute – well, perhaps two because he was really big – Kragg was ***securely bound*** and being dragged towards the Time Trolley. Shakespeare approached from the other direction, pulling Proteus along by one of his ankles.

'**Well, it's been quite a year,**' said the voice of Hattie, the onboard computer.

'What do you mean, a year?' asked Angus. 'It's been, like, a couple of hours.'

'**Still not quite got his head around time travel, has he?**' Hattie asked the world in general. '**There's been quite a lot of work going on behind the scenes, you know. Future Marge and I spent *ages* inventing this new trolley, then planning that diversion.**' The words 'future Marge' hit Angus like a train to the gut, which is extremely uncomfortable – don't under any circumstances try it at home. The fact that he'd just seen his friend hit by a laser blast and completely destroyed seemed too big to fit inside his head.

'**Come on, then, slowcoaches,**' said Hattie encouragingly. '**Remember what Marge told you?**'

'Get Kragg and Proteus back to Hyper-Buy?' Angus recalled. 'But . . . why?'

'**You'll find out when you get there, won't you?**' Hattie replied bafflingly. '***Hurry up!*** **Dictator and sidekick on board, please. We will be departing for the Age of the Idiot in precisely thirty seconds.**'

'Don't we need to get you up to eight miles an hour?' asked Angus as Bloodclaw, Emmeline and Shakespeare managed to wrestle Kragg's enormous, unconscious form into the trolley followed by the limp and meek Proteus.

'**Nah,**' Hattie told him. '**This is the *new improved model* with a better battery. Hold on tight, time pirates. Here . . . we . . . go!**' And, with a flash of multicoloured rainbow flames, which will also look really amazing in the film, the trolley vanished.

As the Time Trolley flew back through the soft purple light of the chill-out zone, the calming route between different periods of time, the occupants sat in stunned silence. Kragg was quite literally stunned – the rest of them were stunned by what had just happened. Angus simply couldn't believe that Marge was gone. The thought that he was travelling through time without her was so huge that he felt like his head couldn't contain it. McQueen, tucked under his arm, whimpered sadly.

'It'll be OK,' said Akila softly, touching him on the shoulder. He reached up and briefly held her hand, but as he gazed out into the endless void he really felt that nothing would ever truly be OK ever again.

'She was the best and the fiercest non-Viking I ever met,' said Bjorn Bloodclaw. 'I bet she's drinking an enormous horn of mead in Valhalla right now.'

'With some cheese on the side,' added Emmeline Pankhurst with a faint, watery smile.

'**Hang on, kids,**' announced Hattie. '**We are approaching the Age of the Idiot. I can feel myself growing slightly stupider by the millisecond. Brace yourselves for re-entry and plot twist.**'

'Plot twist?' repeated Angus faintly. And at that moment there was a sparking, a blatting and a large ***FWOOSH*** as the trolley re-materialized back in the supermarket car park of Hyper-Buy. It was dark, and it took Angus's eyes a few moments to readjust to the gloom. But when they did so, he understood what Hattie had been talking about when she had mentioned a plot twist. Because there, parked neatly beneath one of the street lights, was the Time Trolley – the cool future Time Trolley with the coloured lights. Sitting inside the trolley were two people. And **both** of them were Marge.

'Fwep,' said Angus intelligently. 'Peh . . . peh . . . what?' Even Akila, he was relieved to see, was looking at him rather blankly as they climbed out of the trolley. One of the twin Marges in the second Time Trolley was wearing the shiny silver jumpsuit – clearly she was the version they'd just seen get disintegrated in Ancient Egypt. The other was their old familiar friend. 'Jelly baby?' she called, reaching into her trouser pocket as she clambered out of her own trolley and walked over to join them.

'Meng . . .' said Angus. 'Fwip. Hhhhuh?'

'I think he's asking what on earth is going on?' said Akila helpfully.

'You got shot!' babbled Angus, suddenly regaining the power of speech. 'We just watched you get shot.'

Marge shook her head. 'Not me, dear. Her.' She jerked a thumb over her shoulder to where the silver-jumpsuit-wearing Marge was standing calmly. 'I wouldn't be caught **dead** in a jumpsuit, dear. Not at my age.'

'So . . . what? Have you gone to the future to . . . clone yourself or something?' Angus wanted to know.

'*Clone* myself? I think you've been watching too many science-fiction films.' Marge chuckled. 'Besides, what kind of a monster would that make me? Create another version of myself, then send it back into the past just so she could get shot? Imagine!' She shook her head. 'No, no. I just popped to my lab in the ninety-ninth century to soup up the trolley a bit, then nipped to the shops and bought a **DinnerBot**. Show him, Marge.' The Marge in the silver jumpsuit obediently grabbed itself by the hair and pulled upward. The entire top of its head came away, revealing a tangle of wires with a spinning, glowing orb at the centre.

'It's . . . a ***robot?***' asked Angus weakly.

'Yes, I told you. A DinnerBot,' replied actual Marge. 'Very popular in the future. If you're invited to a dinner party and you can't be bothered to go, you send a DinnerBot in your place. They look very realistic. The artificial intelligence isn't very advanced, but it's more than capable of dealing with the conversation at a dinner party. Right, DinnerBot. Ready?'

'You have a ***lovely*** home,' replied the DinnerBot. 'Where's your floor from?'

'Yes, well,' said Marge. 'That's quite enough of that. Time to be our decoy. Happy landings!' And she pushed the Time Trolley away down the car park. Gaining speed rapidly on its new improved wheels, it began to spark and glow, vanishing into the past just as the DinnerBot was saying, 'This is delicious! You must let me have the recipe.'

'Well, that was a risky plan,' complained Emmeline Pankhurst from the Time Trolley behind Angus, where she was keeping an eye on the still-unconscious Kragg and the cowering Proteus. 'You've just sent that eclectic lady back to the battle to provide a diversion – just ***assuming*** we'll be able to overpower Kragg and defeat him?'

'I didn't have to assume anything, Emmeline, dear,' Marge explained. 'I ***know*** you'll be able to overpower Kragg and bring him back here. I've just seen you arrive with him unconscious. There he is, right there!' she pointed.

'Time travel messes with my head,' moaned Angus, not for the last time.

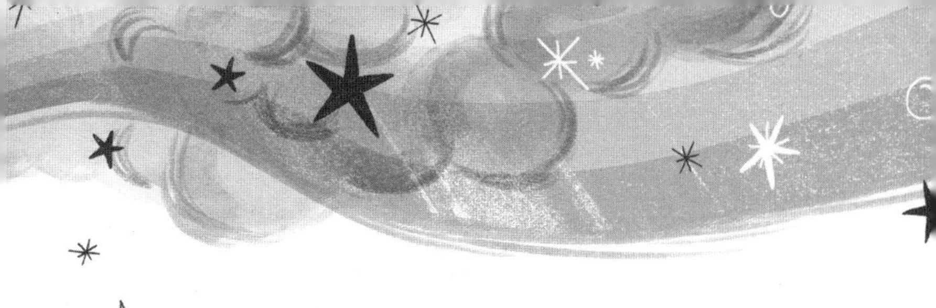

CHAPTER 19

YOU AND HALLOUMI GOT A WHOLE LOT OF HISTORY

'So, now do you understand it?' asked Marge for the seventh time, five minutes later. Angus, Emmeline, Bloodclaw and Shakespeare all shook their heads.

Akila nodded enthusiastically, her hair braid bobbing as she did so. 'It's ***obvious***, isn't it?' she said.

'Not to everyone, apparently,' Marge went on. 'Look, I'll explain it all one last time.'

Akila clicked her fingers. 'I think I can help,' she said. 'Will, hand me a bit of parchment, would you?' Shakespeare obligingly handed over a sheet of yellowish paper, and Angus fished in his pocket for a pen.

'Right,' said Marge. 'Pay attention this time.' And,

with Akila drawing a diagram to make things a little easier, she explained the Time Trolley's journey.

'Kragg stole the trolley, imprisoned me in the medieval dungeon and ended up in Ancient Egypt,' she said. 'But I stole it back off him after the chariot race, remember? And I disappeared?' They nodded. Angus understood this first part, but after that things had got a little confusing. 'I went to the ninety-ninth century,' said Marge. 'And I sent the trolley back to the Age of the Idiot . . . **empty**.'

'And it was by the clock tower!' Angus's face brightened as he – apologies for this – clocked on.

'Yes! Finally he gets it!' Marge smiled and offered her bag of jelly babies round once again. 'Meanwhile I stayed in the ninety-ninth century and **invented** the new improved trolley. That took about a year. Then I reinstalled Hattie, bought a DinnerBot and came back here to wait for you.'

Akila took up the story: 'We got the original Time Trolley from the town hall roof and rescued Marge from the medieval castle. We picked up Will, Emmeline and Bjorn and came here to confront Kragg. We chased him to

Ancient Egypt –' she drew a long arrow from right to left on the parchment – 'where the Time Trolley was destroyed.' She added a small explosion hieroglyph to her diagram.

'That's right, dear,' Marge told her with a grin. 'Then, once I knew you'd defeated Kragg, I sent DinnerBot back to create the distraction. And here we all are!'

'And I thought my plots were complicated,' said Shakespeare with a sigh. 'This makes my newly bald head ache.'

'And now we're almost done,' said Marge in a satisfied tone. 'Time to drop Kragg and Proteus off with the police in the ninety-ninth century and take you lot home. Then I think it's time for a cup of tea. I'd ***kill*** for a lovely cup of tea right now. Not literally, dear,' she added, seeing that Bloodclaw was reaching for one of his axes. 'Right, Hattie,' she declared. 'Take us home, please. And tell the police we're on the way.'

We're not sure what it is about supervillains, but they never seem to properly admit that they've been defeated, do they? Instead of going: 'It's a fair cop, you win. I'm clearly the baddie and I congratulate you on your victory,' they say stuff like, 'I shall return!' or, 'You may have won this round, but you haven't seen the last of me.'

'***I shall return!***' bellowed evil Emperor Kragg as they dumped him out of the Time Trolley in front of a huge ring of ninety-ninth-century police officers pointing disintegration cannons at him. 'You may have won this round, but you haven't seen the last of me! ***Bwa-ha-haa***.'

Marge sighed. 'I just knew he was going to say something like that,' she told her friends.

'We shall meet again, Marganulus Five,' continued Kragg gloatingly. 'For one day in the future, I shall ***destroy you!***'

'That only just happened,' Marge replied, deadpan. 'And it wasn't in the future, it was in the past.'

'Oh, yes,' said Kragg, looking confused. 'Time travel plays havoc with your tenses, doesn't it?'

(As the authors of a time-travel adventure, this is the first time we have agreed with anything Kragg has said.)

'It really does,' agreed Angus, helping Emmeline Pankhurst dump Doctor Proteus beside his boss.

'Well, we must be going,' said Marge. 'You just stay here and ***go to prison*** for the rest of your life, all right? Officers, Hattie's uploaded her recordings of what this villain's been up to.' (Yes, she's a powerful computer but she also has very impressive 360-degree dashcam recording equipment.) 'You should have all the evidence you need to put him away. Cheerio, now. Hattie, set course for . . . Who wants to go home first?'

'I should get back to my good lady Anne,' said Shakespeare, with a glance at Akila. 'I fear I should be more help around the house. Also, I've had a great idea for a play.' Emmeline Pankhurst rolled her eyes. 'I was planning to do some Roman stories,' he mused, once again running a hand over his newly bald scalp, 'but our chariot race gave me an idea.'

'Ooh, are you going to write an Egyptian one?' asked Akila, sounding excited.

'Why not both?' he replied. 'How about *Antony . . . and Cleopatra*? Both on stage together? That's quite a double bill! Double . . . ***bill***. Get it? Because my name's William, you see . . .' But fortunately he was prevented from any further Elizabethan wit by the Time Trolley dematerializing and flying backwards through the void, preparing to drop Marge's team of time heroes back to their own home epochs. ***Epochs*** is a good word, isn't it? In fact, why don't you try and sneak it into conversations with some grown-ups? They won't know what to do. Even better, record yourself doing it and get someone to put it online with the hashtag ISaidEpochToAnAdult.

As you'd expect after such an adventure through time, there were some very emotional farewells as Marge's time army disbanded. Bjorn Bloodclaw folded them all in a rough bear hug as they said their goodbyes on a windswept beach, with his band of Vikings looking on in hairy bewilderment. 'I've left you a ***massive*** pack of Puppy Soft in the longship, dear,' Marge called out from the trolley in farewell, earning herself a gigantic roar of triumph from the whole crew.

Emmeline Pankhurst, meanwhile, took an extra few minutes to talk to Akila as they dropped her back in 1904. 'You really are a most impressive young lady,' the suffragette told her.

'Back atcha,' replied Akila, who had picked up some Idiot Age slang. 'Keep **fighting**, won't you?'

'Always,' replied Emmeline with a wink. 'You too. It's a battle for the ages, you know.'

'Deal,' replied Akila with a firm handshake.

'Just a couple more stops,' Marge told the others as Hattie set course for the early seventeenth century.

'Have you brought that no-good wastrel of a husband back?' screeched Anne Hathaway through the window of her cottage. 'It's about time!'

'It really is about time, dear,' enthused Shakespeare, climbing out of the trolley and accidentally stepping on one of the flower beds. 'And it's given me a simply superb idea for a play. You see, there's this incredible woman from the future . . . and she travels in a magical chariot that can pass between different periods of history . . .'

'Sounds rubbish,' his wife retorted. 'I've told you, give the people what they want. Put a jester and funny butler in it.'

'Actually,' mused Shakespeare, with a glance at Akila, 'I've got some great ideas about Ancient Egypt.'

'Who's going to go and see ***that?***' said Anne scornfully, disappearing inside her cottage and slamming the door.

'Well . . .' Shakespeare turned back to the only three people now left in the Time Trolley. Solemnly, he shook hands with Angus, Akila and Marge. 'Our revels now are ended,' he told them sadly. 'And, like this insubstantial pageant faded . . .'

'Get in here and pull your weight for once!' yelled the voice from the open window. 'I'll give you an insubstantial pageant, you lazy puffy-trousered ***coxcomb!***'

'No idea how I'm going to explain the hair,' said Shakespeare nervously before giving them a final grin and disappearing through the cottage door.

'Now, then,' said Marge. 'There really is just one more stop to make.' She turned to face Akila. 'Ready to go home, dear?'

'Actually, no,' said Akila. 'I think I'd like to do just one more thing, if that's possible.'

'Well,' said Marge doubtfully, 'I suppose you have been very helpful. What did you have in mind?'

'I would like,' said Akila, catching Angus's eye and breaking into a grin, 'to finish my exchange visit to Angus's house, please. After all,' she added, 'I think his history presentation is going to be worth listening to, don't you?'

Angus's face broke into a wide grin and McQueen gave a delighted yip of agreement.

*

'I've got to be honest,' said Angus Roberts four days later, 'until a few weeks ago I wasn't that interested in history. I actually thought it was ***incredibly boring***.' Beside him, he saw the head teacher look sharply in his direction. The hall full of parents shifted uncomfortably. This wasn't the kind of speech about history lessons they'd been expecting to hear at the school open evening. But Angus wasn't bothered what they thought. His eyes rested on the four people sitting right before him on the front row: Akila (with McQueen curled up comfortably in her lap), Marge, and his mum and dad. They were all looking at him proudly. His mum and dad knew Marge from the supermarket, but they'd been a bit ***surprised*** when Angus had told them she was coming along. 'She's been helping me with my homework,' was his entirely honest reply to their questions.

'I always thought history was about kings and queens, and long-ago battles and a load of stuff that didn't make any difference,' Angus went on. 'But you know what's amazing about history, once you realize it? It's actually about real people. Ordinary people. People who were kind, and brave, and funny.' He caught Akila's eye as she beamed at him. 'And that's the really interesting stuff about history,' he continued. 'Not the kings and queens. The way people acted in their everyday lives. I love finding out, you know . . . how they spoke. What made them laugh. What **cheese** they liked to eat.' There was a ripple of laughter. 'And how they looked out for each other,' Angus went on. 'You can learn a lot by travelling through time. You can meet some really, really brilliant people. Not just famous people like, I don't know . . . Shakespeare. Or Emmeline Pankhurst. Though they're both really cool. But there are people from history who are even more brilliant.'

And at this point, just for a moment, Angus allowed his mind to wander back over the last few days of Akila's visit. They had eaten fish-finger sandwiches. They had played endless games of chess. They had wandered around Hyper-Buy, with his friend marvelling at the goods on display. And most of all, they had **talked**. Talked for hours about how their lives were going to turn out: what they wanted to do, and be, and become. And he felt a tug on his heart as he decided that he may well have just made the best friend he would ever have in his life – and they were about to be separated forever. Because, as soon as this presentation was over, Marge had

made him ***promise*** that they would drop Akila back in Ancient Egypt. And then she was going to dismantle the Time Trolley completely. It was too big a risk – there was always the chance that Kragg would escape in the far future and come looking for it. The only safe course was to put it out of action for all time.

'These people are separated from us by hundreds or even thousands of years,' said Angus, feeling a lump forming in his throat but forcing himself to go on. 'But once you get to know them, you realize that there's more that unites us than there is separating us. If you look at it the right way, history is full of new friends.

And that's why it's now my ***favourite*** subject.' The head teacher began clapping his large hands together at enormous volume, rising to his feet with a gigantic smile on his face. And the whole hall followed suit, clapping enthusiastically as Angus felt himself blushing scarlet.

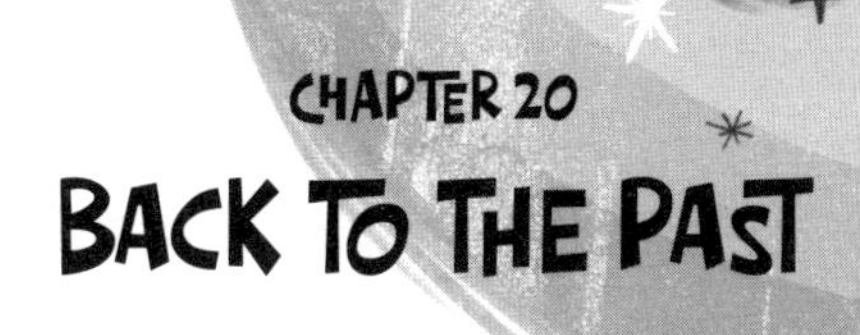

CHAPTER 20
BACK TO THE PAST

Half an hour later, Angus, Akila and Marge stood in the car park. His parents, after many hugs and proud words about his presentation, and also after promising him pizza when he got home, had said goodbye to Akila and Marge. It would be a double celebration – his mum had landed the promotion she'd been working so hard towards and, in a dramatic gesture, had chucked all her notebooks in the bin. 'I'll have ***much more time*** to hang out with you now,' she'd promised Angus with an apologetic grin.

As far as his parents were concerned, Angus was going to spend a short time saying goodbye before Marge drove the exchange student to the airport. They would have found the truth a little harder to swallow – that the three were about to travel thousands of years into the past and say one last goodbye.

'You're definitely going to bring the dog, are you?' asked Marge doubtfully. She was eyeing McQueen, who was pulling excitedly on his lead.

'Don't worry,' Angus reassured her. 'I'll keep a tight hold on him this time.'

'And there's ***absolutely no chance*** you guys might visit?' asked Akila one last time, reaching down to give the dog a soft stroke.

Marge looked at the Egyptian girl sadly. 'I'm sorry,' she told her. 'But all this has made me realize one thing. As long as this time machine exists, Kragg's going to be a threat. And not just Kragg. Who knows who else might want to use it for their own ends? No, it's no good.' She reached out and gave the side of the trolley a fond little pat. 'I was kidding myself that I could just hide away and pop backwards and forwards collecting cheese. You saw what almost happened just then. I put the whole of time at risk. So, we really haven't got any . . . er, ***time*** to lose, I'm afraid. We need to take you home, come back to the Age of the Idiot . . . and then it's goodbye, Time Trolley. There's really nothing else for it.'

'I wish there was another way,' said Angus, a tear welling up at the corner of his eye.

Akila reached out and squeezed him on the shoulder, and he could see that she was holding back tears too. 'She's right, you know,' his new friend told him gently. 'It's been brilliant seeing all these odd places, but I really don't belong anywhere else. This is the way it's got to be. Or, at least, the way it's going to have to have been . . . Well, you know what I mean.' Sadly, Angus nodded.

'Hattie,' he said, 'set course for Akila's home time, please.'

'**Ancient Egypt it is,**' the computer confirmed, sounding slightly choked up. '**Sorry,**' she added. '**I'm just *terrible* at goodbyes.**'

'Yeah,' agreed Angus as the trolley began to glow in preparation for one final time jump. 'Me too.'

The sun beat down on the desert and flicked dazzling specks of reflected light from the rippled river that ran beside the lost city of Thonis. And as the afternoon just began to fade into evening, three weary travellers approached the outskirts, trudging down a steep dune towards the wooden bridge that led towards the marketplace.

'Feels good to be home,' said Akila in a satisfied tone, looking around her and sniffing the air. 'I wonder whether they've started cleaning up from the dramatic chariot race and subsequent ***laser battle*** in the market square.'

'Ah, well . . .' Marge looked slightly shifty. 'I checked on that with Hattie. Because her guidance systems were slightly off, that actually isn't due to happen for another 234 years. So you're probably OK.'

'Oh, right.' Akila thought about this for a moment. 'Good to know that Keket's Rope Stall will still be going, though. I thought the shopkeeper looked unfamiliar. Must be one of Keket's great-great-great-grandchildren.' She shrugged, and Angus was impressed once again by how easily Akila seemed to have grasped the concept of time travel. The whole thing still made his brain feel like a shaken-up can of fizzy drink – he didn't want to open it too quickly in case it exploded right in his face.

'Here we are, then. This is where we first met, isn't that right, dear?' Marge stopped at the other end of the bridge, near the wharves where several boats were tied up.

'This is it,' confirmed Akila. 'Well –' she looked Angus in the eye – 'I guess this is goodbye, then.'

Angus felt more tears pricking at the edges of his eyes. 'I've got something for you,' he blurted, feeling like he needed to speak quickly before he started crying properly. Fumbling in his back pocket, he pulled out a copper bracelet with the letter A embossed on it – the one he'd accidentally taken from the market stall in Roman Britain on his very first trip through time.

'I'll think of my friend whenever I wear it,' Akila told him seriously as she placed it on her wrist. 'And –' she blinked back a few tears herself – 'I'll wear it ***every single day*** of my life.'

Angus now felt like there was too much pressure in his chest to speak properly. 'But . . . how will I know you are – were – OK?' he asked eventually. 'I'll be worried about you.'

'Hey – I'll be fine.' Akila gave his arm a comforting squeeze. 'If there's ever a way to get a message to you, I will. But I don't suppose there will be. And listen, you take care of yourself, future boy. It's far more dangerous where you come from, surrounded by all those idiots, than it is here.'

'***Five minutes* to temporal resolve,**' said Hattie through their earpieces.

'Which reminds me, dear,' said Marge. 'I'll need that back, I'm afraid.' She pointed to the earpiece that was translating for Akila. With a nod, Akila pulled it from her ear and handed it over.

'Bye, then,' said Angus.

'*Echket t'cha mabis*,' Akila replied. Without Hattie's help, they could no longer communicate. But, with a shrug, she stepped forward and hugged them both before giving McQueen's furry head one final ruffle.

And that, at least, needed no translation.

With one last, sad smile, Akila turned and vanished into the bustling crowds of Thonis. A city that, by the time Angus would be born, would have been lost beneath the sea for centuries.

'Come on, dear.' Marge folded an arm around his shoulders and led him back across the bridge. '***Home time***.' And Angus, picking up McQueen and feeling his warm, comforting weight beneath his arm, followed her, leaving his friend Akila behind forever.

For one last time, the Time Trolley touched down smoothly in the Hyper-Buy car park. Marge looked around her with a satisfied sigh. 'Well, we're back,' she said. 'I must say, I'll miss ***Marge's Army***. I wonder whether William ever did write that play about time travel? It went missing somewhere along the way, if so. Probably for the best. I mean, whoever would have believed it?'

'**Timelines resolved,**' said Hattie. '**Destination achieved. Welcome back to the Age of the Idiot.**' Automatically, Angus looked round for Akila and felt a sharp stab of regret to see that her usual place just beside him in the trolley was vacant. The sudden thought came to him that she had now lived her entire life thousands of years ago. He would never hear from her, ever again. And she had been, he was now firmly convinced, the best friend he would ever have.

'So, seriously?' asked Angus as he climbed out. 'No more time travel ever?'

'No more time travel, ever,' confirmed Marganulus Five, inventor from the far future and the greatest cheese historian the planet will ever know. 'This really is the end.'

'Does that mean you're staying here?' asked Angus. 'Here in the ***Age of the Idiot?***' he emphasised with a smile.

'Well,' Marge looked around her. 'I've become quite fond of the place, you know. I'll miss that ancient British cheese, though. And I think Menneth will miss the toilet paper. Ah well.'

'I'd just love to know she was OK,' said Angus, thinking back to Akila disappearing into the busy crowds of Thonis and remembering about a thousand things he wished he'd been able to say to her.

Marge looked thoughtful for a moment. 'You never know,' she said finally. 'Maybe there's ***some other way*** to find out.' She grasped the handle of the Time Trolley and began to push it into her workshop at the back of the supermarket, ready to begin dismantling it and putting it out of Kragg's reach forever.

'But how?' said Angus. 'How would I be able to get a message from somebody who lived thousands of years ago?'

'Oh, I don't know,' said Marge casually. By now the trolley was in the workshop and her final words came through the doors just before they closed.

'Maybe you'll work something out . . .

. . . in time.'

THE END.

KARK! Hello, it's the Chief Puffin here. I'm aware that my idiotic authors have left the end of this story on an enormous cliffhanger. And, as a bird who lives on a cliff top, I absolutely hate cliffhangers. So I've flown here with my weirdly small wings to tell them to add another bit at the end telling us what happens next. **KARK!**

OK, Chief Puffin. So you want a postscript or epilogue to this book?

KARK! Don't be so pretentious. Just call it an extra bit at the end.

Fine, fine. Extra bit at the end coming up.

KARK! Thank you. Now I shall return to my burrow and have my tea.

Is it ***fish?***

No, it's lasagne.

Really?

No, of course not, you fools. I'm a **PUFFIN**. I don't have thumbs. How would I possibly layer sheets of pasta, béchamel sauce and ragù in order to make a lasagne?

Well, maybe you ordered a ***takeaway.***

I just told you, I don't have **THUMBS!** Also I'm a **BIRD**. So no, I did not order a takeaway. I'm eating a fish for my tea. Just a raw fish.

Ah, yes. ***Very good.*** You really had us going there, Chief Puffin.

GET ON WITH IT!

Sorry. Right. Yes. Enjoy your raw fish. Here we go.

EXTRA BIT AT THE END

That's better.

Twenty years later . . .

Ooh, cool. **KARK!**

Quiet now, please, Chief Puffin. Listen to the end of the story.

The sunlight reflected back from the calm surface of the blue ocean in a countless array of dazzling diamonds. In the distance, high dunes and tall buildings marked the Egyptian coastline. But here, half a mile offshore, a large boat pitched smoothly on the gently rippling water. On the wide open deck at the back, figures clustered around a screen, sheltered from the sun by a canvas awning. The screen was showing a live feed from the robot submarine that was diving deep beneath the surface, exploring the caverns and gullies that lay beneath the water.

'The ancient city of **Thonis** was a thriving port and a centre for industry, trade and fishing,' said a voice on deck. Behind the crowd clustered at the screen stood a TV presenter, dressed in a wetsuit and scuba gear, with his face mask pushed up on his forehead. He was making a documentary about the search for this incredible lost city.

'That's it!' said a voice from the crowd clustered around the screen. 'We're through!' The presenter edged forward.

'Let's see if we can grab a quick word with the leader of this amazing underwater journey of discovery,' he said. '**Professor of Egyptology**, Angus Roberts.

Professor Roberts, you've spent years researching the lost city of Thonis-Heracleion. It must have been a fascinating place.'

Angus turned away from the screen for a moment, memories filling his mind. Memories of a crocodile swimming lazily beneath a bridge. Of McQueen running away through the bustling streets. And of his best friend's smile. 'Fascinating indeed,' he agreed. 'Terrible **cheese**, though.'

The documentary host gave the nervous laugh of someone who suspects they've just missed out on a clever joke. 'And your submarine has finally discovered the part of the city you've been searching for?' he asked.

'Have a look,' said Angus, turning back to the screen. His scientific team parted to let him get a better view. After all, he was the foremost authority on the history of Thonis. The camera feed from the sub was now showing eerie footage of a gigantic statue.

'We call her the Dark Queen,' Angus explained as he pointed towards the faded, solemn bust of the late monarch, submerged in the ocean. 'She once stood in the main square of Thonis. The scene of many amazing things.' He smiled at some memory. 'And for the first time,' he went on, 'we're going to try and take the sub right into one of the buildings that once stood nearby.' The submarine camera was now travelling down a deep, dark underwater ravine. 'Thousands of years ago,' Angus explained, 'this was one of the streets of the ancient city of Thonis. And just the other day, my team made an ***incredible discovery***, right here.' And now, powerful spotlights on the front of the sub activated, illuminating a narrow archway, half buried in the seabed and almost covered by waving fronds of weeds. Carefully, the sub was guided through the opening.

'We are seeing this sight for the first time in nearly two thousand years,' exclaimed Angus softly, bending forward to peer intently at the screen. The spotlights were now illuminating a large wall, covered from top to bottom with elaborate carvings. The spotlight moved across birds, what looked like an eye with three legs, an owl, a stag, a scarab beetle, a shepherd with a crook . . . 'This is it!' whispered Angus. 'This is where ***she*** –' he stopped himself – 'I mean,' he went on, 'these carvings indicate that a wealthy family lived here. Thanks to the fact that this ancient writing was finally decoded in the last couple of decades, we can actually read the messages that these long-ago people left here.'

'This is really fascinating, and very mysterious,' said the TV presenter, looking over Angus's shoulder. 'This carving here, for instance. What would that represent? Some sort of chariot?'

Professor Angus Roberts turned away from the camera, so the documentary crew didn't see his eyes had filled with tears. '***A chariot?***' he said softly. 'Yes . . . a chariot. Marge, are you seeing this?' One of his team moved to stand by his side, an older woman with curly hair that was beginning to turn grey.

'Oh, you found it at last,' she said in a voice filled with emotion. 'You clever, clever boy. You found it.'

'It almost looks like a modern-day shopping trolley, doesn't it?' said the presenter excitedly. 'How fascinating! And do we know anything about what that ***writing*** beside it might say?'

By now the submarine had backed off slightly, and its floodlight was illuminating the entire panel. Next to the carving of what did indeed look very much like a shopping trolley were a series of carved figures. The two people closest to the trolley were the smallest, and beside them was a small carving of a dog. The stone was old and worn, but the bracelet on the wrist of one of the pair was clearly visible. Next to them was a long line of hieroglyphs.

'It says . . .' Angus leaned in to make out the ancient writing. 'This is the chariot of my **best friend**. And this is our army. I want to tell you that I'm happy. And don't spend too much time **looking back**. You're right where you're supposed to be.'

'Perhaps a little snippet of Ancient Egyptian poetry?' the presenter asked, looking confused. He gave another small, nervous laugh. 'I think it's safe to say that no one will ever know what that really means.'

'I wouldn't bank on it,' said Marge softly, glancing at Angus with tears glistening in her eyes.

ORDINARY KIDS.

EXTRAORDINARY ADVENTURES.

LAUGHS FOR THE WHOLE FAMILY!

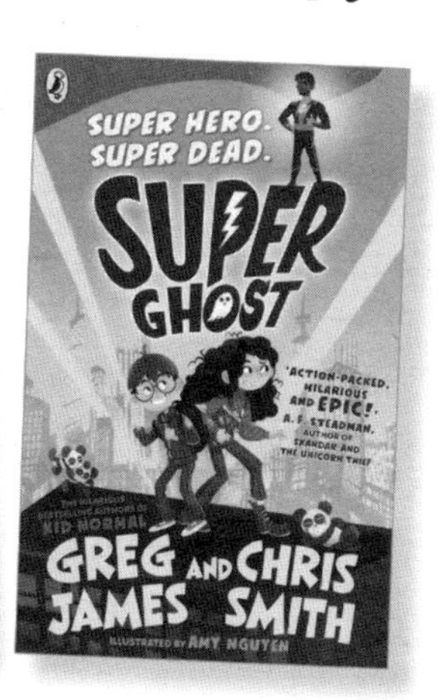

From the incredible imagination of

CHRIS SMITH . . .